Heart of Wisdom

We come and go like grass, which in the morning shoots up and in the evening fades and withers The number of our years may be many or few, so teach us to number our days that we may grow a heart of wisdom.

—From the 90th Psalm

Heart of Wisdom

Alan N. Clifford

Lion Publishers
New York, NY

Editorial, Sales, and Customer Service

Lion Publishers
alan.n.clifford@gmail.com

Copyright © 2013 by Alan N. Clifford

All rights reserved. No part of the material protected by this copyright notice may be reproduced or utilized in any form, electronic or mechanical, including photocopying, recording, or by any information storage and retrieval system, without written permission from the copyright owner.

Library of Congress Control Number: 2013930477

ISBN 13: 978-0-9888597-0-8 (alk. paper)

Any resemblance in this book to characters living or dead is purely coincidental.

Printed in the United States of America
17 16 15 14 13   10 9 8 7 6 5 4 3 2 1

For JKC with thanks to CM

PROLOGUE

November 1970

Ten-year-old Paul Bergman was fascinated by the grainy black and white images of twentieth-century warfare as he sat with his family and watched a Thanksgiving TV special celebrating the 25th anniversary of the end of World War II. Grouped around the TV set in the living room with him were his parents, as well as uncles, aunts, cousins, and grandparents. Some paid attention to the TV show, some chatted. The younger cousins played on the floor. They had just consumed their holiday dinner: turkey, stuffing, and all the traditional side dishes. Some of the older family members were already beginning to nod off, but not Paul and the younger children. For Paul, this was an especially poignant documentary, for while his father—white-haired and serious in demeanor—had been kept out of military service by a residual limp from childhood polio, his father's two younger and more talkative brothers, Uncle Ted and Uncle Bob, had been in the Army. Both had seen combat. Although they were normally reluctant to go into detail about their experiences, they were particularly interested in the newsreel coverage of the places they had been while in uniform. Paul asked them questions as the various campaigns were described on TV and they answered as best they could. The boy's knowledge surprised them.

"Sounds like you might become a history major when you get to college, Paulie," Uncle Bob said, with a gentle laugh that seemed almost out of place coming from such a stocky body.

"I want to become a doctor," the boy said. "I want to help people get well when they're sick, but I sure do love reading about all the famous wartime battles. Where did you and Uncle Ted spend most of your time as soldiers?"

"We were in what was called the Pacific Theater of Operations," Uncle Ted answered this time, "but not in the same area. We were in infantry units, we saw friends get killed. It wasn't pretty. Hey, look—there are some newsreels of the big naval battle in Leyte Gulf in the Philippines. You may have heard about that one."

Everyone looked on dutifully as scenes of the lopsided American naval victory flashed before them on the TV, followed by the unopposed landing on the beaches with General MacArthur up to his ankles in the surf while photographers snapped away, and finally the liberation of Japanese POW camps. The latter pictures dampened the festive holiday mood because the surviving Americans pictured there were stick-like remnants of their former selves.

"Who are those skinny guys?" Paul asked his father, who was sitting quietly between his two brothers on the couch. His father again deferred to Uncle Ted.

Uncle Ted's tone was somber. "Those are Americans from the Bataan Death March in 1942 who managed to survive nearly three more years in Japanese prison camps. They are true American heroes, Paulie, because the Japanese were especially brutal to them." His eyes misted. "I saw some of them after their liberation. Pathetic. They looked like the pictures of Holocaust survivors, like our relatives in Germany must have looked when they were freed. We Jews can really identify with them."

"So if you ever have the chance to meet those Bataan survivors, tip your hat to them," said Uncle Bob, interrupting his brother. "Treat them well, they deserve it."

Paul thought about that for a minute before answering, "Not much chance of that, I guess."

"You never know," his father said, suddenly animated. "Life is funny that way. If you really want to be a doctor, Paulie, you're going to take a journey with lots of turns and twists, and you're going to meet all sorts of people, along the way. All sorts."

It sounded interesting, Paul thought, already eager to get started.

CHAPTER

1

July 1989

It was his father's advice that led Bergman to College Station, Massachusetts. Although he had decided to become a cardiologist while still in medical school, it was only during his internship year in New York City that he first became aware of Leo Miller's name. It seemed that almost every time he picked up a cardiology journal there was an article, review, or editorial with Miller's name on it.

Miller, the famous medical research scientist at the University of Western Massachusetts ran high-powered clinical and animal research laboratories whose purpose was to unravel the mysteries of heart attacks and yet at the same time, according to news stories, he retained such a personal rapport with his clinical patients that they sang his praises from one end of the country to the other. When Bergman's father heard his son describing Miller's accomplishments with such evident reverence he asked his son simply, "Why not apply for a fellowship with him? You don't have to be in New York for all of your training."

"It's not that easy to get accepted into his program."

"So? Nothing ventured, nothing gained. Try it, and if you're lucky you'll be sitting at the feet of the master himself."

His father's words made Bergman apply to Miller's program, and when he received his letter of acceptance several months later, Bergman had to restrain himself from running out of his apartment on 88th Street and yelling his good news to all the other inhabitants of Manhattan. He had decided that a fellowship with Miller meant the opportunity to receive high-quality training in clinical cardiology while at the same time being exposed to some of the most exciting developments in scientific research. Bergman could hardly wait for his second year of residency training to end, and when it did on June 30th, he left Manhattan with great excitement.

Driving north from the city, he could feel the temperature drop perceptibly as the hours went by and the suburbs gradually turned into upstate farmland and then the Berkshire Mountain range. Crossing the New York state line into Massachusetts, he made his way through the lush summer countryside past North Windham and then East Windham and eventually drove into College Station, a sleepy mill town by a river, the town where the university and its medical school were located. He had rented a furnished room in a building owned by the hospital—it was certainly a far cry from a studio apartment in one of Manhattan's towers—but he was a bachelor with Spartan needs and it suited him perfectly. Although he had little to unpack, it was nearly midnight by the time he was through, and he fell into bed exhausted.

Bergman awakened a few minutes after 7 a.m. on a comfortably warm July 1st, the traditional beginning of the new year in academic medicine. Within the hour Bergman was one of four men gathered expectantly in the conference room of the cardiology section, a rectangular room paneled in pine with shelving for books and journals. In the middle of the room sat a circular table with folding chairs.

The four new fellows were arrayed in various poses of contrived relaxation, scrutinizing each other carefully while exchanging pleasantries. Gus Adopolous had driven all night from Ohio to be there on time—his eyelids drooped as the minutes wore on; Bill Douglas, was an ebony-colored Georgian, whose speech was slow and measured; Mel Barnes, well-tanned, was an almost too handsome Californian; and Paul Bergman, the serious New Yorker, was taller than the others and sported already thinning brown hair. Adopolous and Barnes were married, Douglas and Bergman were bachelors. No longer medical students nor house officers, they had reached the final level of training. They were smart and knew it, but they were not sure how they would fare under Miller's reputedly stern hand.

The four of them didn't have to wait long to find out. He arrived at five past the hour, greeting them warmly. Leo Miller was a tall man, somewhat heavy but carrying the weight well. His curly gray hair, fierce mustache—gray but heavily speckled with black—and hawk-like nose made him seem like a caricature of an Afghan warrior. At 65, he still exuded an aura of energy and self-confidence. After a few minutes of small talk, he motioned for the new fellows to sit around the table.

"I think you're about to embark on a unique experience," he began after they were all seated, his tone firmer now, one hand pushing back an unruly strand of gray hair that fell over his forehead. "My staff and I will teach you everything we can about cardiology. But there is also something special about being here. You see, it's no secret I've spent a good part of the last 20 years trying to learn why some people die immediately from heart attacks and some don't and what can be done about it. I hope you'll be able to join me in that quest." He paused, as if for dramatic effect, and studied them again before proceeding.

His eyes were perhaps the weakest of his otherwise strong features, yet the fellows still shifted uncomfortably under his gaze. Behind him, a blackboard was cluttered with mathematical symbols, equations, arrows, and diagrams, and Bergman purposely stared at this collection of chalk marks to avoid his scrutiny. It was as if they were raw military recruits and Miller were the drill instructor preparing them for boot camp. Satisfied that they were sufficiently attentive, Miller continued, now carefully stroking his mustache. "To my way of thinking, the search for this particular Holy Grail can be likened to a marathon, not a sprint. Maybe one of you will do something over the course of your fellowship to advance my quest." He stared again at each of them in turn. "If one of you can do that, it will more than compensate my associates and me for the "care and feeding" that we will be expending on you over the next two or three years. I've been doing this for a long time and I say this to every new group of fellows and with very few exceptions they all fail me, but I'm hoping your group will be one of the exceptions." Again, he pushed back the errant locks from his forehead. Seemingly amused by their awe-struck expressions, he allowed the flicker of a smile to cross his features. "Any questions, gentlemen?"

Only Adopolous had the courage to say anything. "What about parking permits? I got kicked out of the hospital lot this morning."

Miller laughed. "I present you with one of the great problems of our times and in response you come up with that trivia? Adopolous, I don't foresee a Nobel Prize in your future."

Adopolous reddened, but did not retreat. "No sir, neither do I. But if I'm going to help you win one, then I've got to have some place to park my car." They all laughed at his retort and the air seemed less charged. Bergman developed an instant liking for this unpretentious Midwesterner.

"Judy," Miller called to one of the secretaries in the outer office, "make sure all of the new fellows have parking permits. And white coats, too, get all of them white coats. Get them long ones, down to their knees, not the jackets. God forbid they should be confused with the medical students; that would really deflate their egos." With a smile, he left. The four fellows looked at each other quizzically.

"Shit! There was no need for him to make me feel like a god-damned fool," Adopolous said, his face still red. "For Christ's sake, I was Phi Beta Kappa and AOA at Ohio State, I'm not a moron."

"I have a feeling membership in honor societies doesn't count for much in Miller's scheme of things," Barnes said in his soft laidback Californian tones. "Let's face it—he's more or less doing you a favor by letting you into his program. He knows it and you know it. That goes for all of us."

Douglas nodded emphatically. "He was playing with you," he drawled, "that's all, don't take it too seriously. I've been a medical student and house officer here, so I know him a little better than the rest of you. Barnes is right, Adopolous, loosen up."

"The only way to console yourself is to think of it as part of a great adventure," Bergman joined in, no longer restrained by Miller's stare. Adopolous didn't agree and said so, but the others understood what Bergman was saying. They got some coffee and talked for a few minutes more.

"Leo Miller is something else," Douglas said, his handsome features breaking into a wide grin. "Don't be put off by his blunt approach."

"Sounds like an open and shut case," Barnes said. "Egomania. Pure and simple."

Douglas' grin grew wider. "You folks don't know Leo Miller very well. Take it from me, nothing's open and shut with him."

Douglas' remarks intrigued Bergman. After all, Douglas said he knew Miller a little better that the rest of them. Was that because he had been at the hospital longer than the others, or was there something else? Before Bergman had a chance to ask, the meeting broke up.

CHAPTER

2

After the first morning of orientation sessions with Miller's staff, the new cardiology fellows went their separate ways, their paths crossing only during the various weekly conferences. Miller had designed his cardiology section's teaching program so that one fellow was assigned to the animal laboratory, one to the cardiac catheterization laboratory, one to the noninvasive station (electrocardiograms, exercise tests, ultrasound examinations of the heart), and the fourth fellow was involved in necessary clinical duties involving the care of Miller's and his faculty associates' private patients. In each rotation, the new first-year fellows were supervised by a staff member; there was usually a second-year fellow around as well.

Bergman requested the animal laboratory as his initial rotation. Because it was summer and the animal laboratory had a reputation for being hot and odoriferous at that time of year, none of the other first-year fellows voiced any objection. Bergman was eager to begin there, since it was in this area of research that he lacked experience, and he thought that the sooner he got started, the better.

In the animal laboratory, Bergman worked with Charlie O'Brien, Miller's chief research associate, his technician, Eddy, and Eric Sanderson, a third-year research fellow. O'Brien was short and thin, Sanderson just the opposite—tall and well-built—but it was Eddy who had the most intriguing appearance. Eddy was a former prize-fighter and had the flattened nose and swollen ears to prove it. Despite his intimidating looks, he was always pleasant and a great source of aid to Sanderson who had been so productive in his research activities during his two-year clinical fellowship that Miller had invited him to stay on for an additional year. This indicated that he was on a fast track for a faculty appointment.

"Do as well as Sanderson," O'Brien told Bergman, "and you'll be a star. Even do half as well, and I'll be impressed."

Bergman immediately plunged into the routine of the laboratory, which was every bit as hot and uncomfortable as advertised. Located in the bowels of the hospital, its air-conditioning unit broke down all too frequently. As junior staff, it was his responsibility to take the dog—a stray acquired from local pounds—out of its cage and to comfort and calm it while Eddy shaved a small area on the foreleg and then quickly inserted an intravenous sedative. After the dog was sedated, Eddy and Bergman would lift it onto the operating table, insert a breathing tube attached to a tank of oxygen, and begin the experiment. They didn't treat the animals as one would a human patient, but they did make it a point to see that the animal was heavily sedated for the procedures (opening the chest and isolating the arteries of the heart) so it would feel no pain.

When Bergman joined the team, O'Brien and Sanderson were in the midst of a series of heart-attack experiments originally designed by Miller several months earlier.

The goal was to find and administer a drug or provide another type of treatment to the animal before, or during, the occlusion of the coronary artery to prevent a fatal outcome. Many such interventions had been tried over the past several months. Each had its drawbacks. The very act of opening the animal's chest to tie off the coronary artery created an artificiality that might skew the outcome. Furthermore, the tie often did not function reliably in causing a heart attack, thus leading to serious problems in analyzing the results.

In addition to the entire day in the laboratory, the work often extended into the evening as well. Bergman lost track of time in this lab setting, even going without meals from time to time. As he became more adept at the experimental protocol, he became inquisitive as to why things were done one way and not another. O'Brien and Sanderson largely ignored his questions as they huddled over the dog, but if Bergman persisted he usually got an answer after the work was completed.

Working in such close cooperation, he also got to know each of his colleagues better, especially O'Brien, who he found to be a fascinating character. Much to Bergman's surprise, he soon learned that this brilliant scientist's hobby was racing sports cars! He had actually placed in several amateur rallies. To anyone who would listen, O'Brien explained that auto racing presented a welcome release from the hours spent either hunched over the animal's open chest or analyzing the mountains of graph paper that were the end product of such experiments. "My lovely dungeon," he called the animal laboratory, but there was no affection in his tone, and, indeed, at times he seemed to act like someone who was serving out a sentence. Every so often, he would explode at Sanderson or Bergman—usually at Bergman during that first month—for some real or imagined mistake that killed a dog prematurely and ruined an otherwise potentially productive experiment.

"Fuck you, Bergman, you asshole!" He was slight of build, and his foul mouth seemed somehow out of place in someone so puny. "An hour to set this dog up just the way I wanted it and you clowns kill it off in thirty seconds. Amazing." With that declaration or some variation thereof, he would rip off his surgical gloves, fling them into a garbage can, and sulk off to his office next door, loudly slamming the door.

"Bergman, you goofed again," said Sanderson, with evident relief that he had been spared O'Brien's ire, at least this time. "Now clean up the mess."

Normally, Eddy would be the one to do this, but when one of the fellows ruined the experiment, O'Brien insisted on the culprit toting the heavy garbage bags himself. Often, by the time they had returned to the laboratory, O'Brien had mellowed somewhat. Sanderson was sure he had liquor sequestered somewhere in the mess of papers and books that littered his small office.

Occasionally, when the routine of the work got to be too much for all of them, O'Brien would invite them to change out of their scrubs and to join him at a neighborhood watering hole for some cold beers. Since the hospital was located in a deteriorating neighborhood, the choice of drinking establishments was limited to a few dark and dirty bars next to fast-food franchises or liquor stores. Settling themselves in a dingy back booth far from the window to avoid accidentally being spotted by some passing hospital employee, O'Brien would treat them to the first round of beer. Unwinding at these "liver rounds" as they were termed for their effects on that particular organ, Bergman came to learn more about Leo Miller than he did during the time spent in the laboratory, where conversation was mostly devoted to shop talk.

"I saw Leo backslapping Wentworth in the cafeteria yesterday," Sanderson announced at one such respite. "I couldn't believe my eyes." Harrison Wentworth was Chief of Medicine and Miller's boss—and ultimately theirs as well. Bergman had heard that Wentworth had a remarkable pedigree both from his New England forebears and also as a result of his college, medical school, and house-staff training. But he had also heard that there was reputed to be bad blood between Wentworth and Miller.

"Hell, Leo does what he has to do to stay afloat," O'Brien replied. "If it was up to Wentworth, Miller would be the one out on his ass, lock, stock, barrel, dogs and you and me, too."

"Why does Wentworth have it in for him?" Bergman asked.

O'Brien frowned. "Look, that's a long story and a complicated one and not for your tender ears."

When O'Brien answered the call of nature and groped through the semi-darkness for the men's room, Bergman turned to Sanderson. "What's the story on Wentworth and Miller?"

"It is the way it's been since I've been at the hospital," Sanderson replied. "Wentworth's well regarded in his field—he wrote a textbook on pulmonary disease—but Leo's demands for more research space, more funding, more staff, and Lord knows what else, must drive Wentworth up the wall. Plus Miller's much more famous, which is the goal of any of us, right? That's enough to explain it. I mean, that's why I'm here. I'm not shy about admitting it. I'm not one of your Albert Schweitzer types," he said with a sneer.

"I guess I'm still idealistic," Bergman admitted.

Sanderson laughed. "You'll learn. By the way how's your love life? We have some hot nurses at the hospital. You interested in the party action?"

Before he could reply, O'Brien returned from the men's room.

"What a filthy disgusting toilet. It's worse than ever," O'Brien said. "Are we ready to return to the dungeon to complete Father Leo's sainthood? No? Thank God, let's have another beer." As they imbibed that round, O'Brien mused pensively about his boss. "Leo's a genius, he really is, but he can get me awfully pissed-off at times."

"Only at times?" Sanderson said. "That puts you in a lot better shape than most of us. Bet he's a tough cookie to live with."

"Hold it right there, Sanderson," O'Brien warned. "Stay out of his personal life." Sanderson withdrew quickly. "Sorry."

"Does he have a problem with his family?" Bergman asked innocently.

"He has no family," O'Brien replied, "just a wife, Arlene, a great lady—a great lady who is also my defender," he added gently, but appeared reluctant to say more. He sat quietly, staring into his beer glass, then, apparently tiring of the beer and the atmosphere, he shoved his glass away and stood up. "Back to the dungeon, men," he announced almost cheerfully. "Let's give it another go for the greater glory of all of us and Father Leo. By the way, we're going to get a visitor this week or next, a big shot from Japan, so stay on your toes."

"What's up?" Sanderson asked.

"I'm not sure, but scuttlebutt has it that our visitor is a cardiologist who's the head of the Japanese Medical Society. He wants to see what we're doing and compare notes with Leo about his own experiments."

"Sounds innocuous enough," Bergman said.

O'Brien paused. "Yes and no. I can't say more. Just make nice."

Later, Bergman would wonder if O'Brien had some misgivings about the impending visit, but for the moment he was only interested in the address for that night's party that Sanderson had slipped into his pocket.

CHAPTER

3

The party was a raucous affair: a small hot apartment, lots of liquor, loud rock music and wall-to-wall male house staff intertwined with student or graduate nurses.

Sanderson spotted Bergman as soon as he came through the door. "Glad you came, rookie. Grab a brewski and then grab some flesh."

Sanderson's face was beet-red with sweat pouring down his neck. He's already drunk, Bergman thought, and decided to avoid him as much as possible. He would just look around a bit, then head home, thinking about tomorrow's early morning experiment in the dog lab.

Surveying the room, Bergman quickly caught the eye of a stunning red-head and made his way through the party-goers to her side.

"Hi," she spoke so softly he had trouble making out her next few words. "I said my name is Vicki. I'm a CCU nurse," she repeated herself, this time more loudly.

"Paul Bergman, first-year cardiology fellow."

She frowned. "Uh-oh, that's not so good."

"Why not?"

"You'll see in about five seconds."

While Bergman puzzled over her remark, he felt someone grab him from behind.

"Not this one, dope. This one belongs to me." Sanderson's hot, sweaty hand was now crushing Bergman's shoulder.

"I don't belong to anyone, Eric," Vicki protested in vain. Sanderson released his grip on Bergman and transferred it to her waist.

"So you say," Sanderson retorted, laughing. As he led her away, he shouted back at Bergman "See you later, dope." The music drowned out the rest of his harangue, which Bergman guessed was not complementary.

"Not a nice way to act, was it?" a woman's voice said with more than a trace of sympathy.

Bergman turned to see a pretty woman with long blond-streaked hair giggling at him. "Sorry for my rudeness," she said, "but that guy needs a kick in the pants."

"Just too much to drink, that's all."

She stuck out her hand. "I'm Jennifer Stein."

"Peter Bergman," he said with a short quick handshake. "Are you a CCU nurse also?"

"Nope, a psychologist from the metabolic research unit on nine west."

"Is that a Boston accent I detect?"

"It is. And what about you? New Yorker?"

"On the money. Family still in Boston?"

"Family is just my mother and father, and you'll be glad to know that all three of us love New York."

"There you go, we're kindred spirits."

He liked her laugh and told her so. "Can we get together some time?"

"Sure, here's my telephone number."

"Great. I'll call you."

"Sounds good, I'll sit by the phone waiting."

They both laughed, and Bergman slipped out of the apartment as unobtrusively as he had entered it.

CHAPTER

4

Leo Miller yawned and stretched his arms and legs. The bedside alarm clock said 6:30 a.m. It was time to get up, to get back to the hospital to his staff and patients and especially to the new group of cardiology fellows, four young men eager to begin learning whatever he could teach them about the human heart and the diseases that afflicted it. But, for the moment, he lay there without moving, wondering whether he still had the desire, after 30-odd years, to repeat this July ritual. Approaching his 66th birthday, his tall somewhat stocky body was showing the wear and tear of his years; the arthritis in his lower spine made every day a potentially painful adventure.

While he lay there reflecting on the coming day, the inert body next to his came to life, sensing he was awake. Thirty years together had trained Arlene Miller's marital antennae to pick up her husband's foreboding with great accuracy. Snuggling closer to him, her body warm and soft against his, she murmured into his ear, "You're wondering whether you really want to do this for another year, right?"

He laughed. "Of course. That's exactly what I'm lying here thinking. Only this year I'm serious about it. That old fire in the belly is not very overwhelming any more. What do you think? Am I foolish to continue?"

Arlene raised her head off the pillow and looked at him skeptically. "Wow. I haven't heard you so down on yourself for a long time. Why quit now?"

"Old age."

Now it was her turn to laugh. "Baloney," she said poking him in the chest. Neither of them wore bed clothes—hadn't since they were married—but his increasingly protuberant belly was in sharp contrast to the still supple contour of her firm breasts. "Come on, get up and go for your morning walk, take your shower, meet the new day. Hey, what's your new group of fellows like?"

"Well, I've got a buckeye."

"What's a buckeye?"

"Ohio State man. That's their mascot, not quite sure whether it's an animal or what."

"Oh."

"And a Californian named Barnes, and of course Douglas from our own house staff. You remember the handsome black resident we had over for dinner several times last year?"

"Yes, I do."

"The fourth one is a New Yorker, Paul Bergman. I have this good feeling about him—could be a sleeper."

"Another one of your hunches?"

Miller smiled. His wife liked to kid him about his "hunches," because they were invariably wrong—except about Sanderson, of course. Miller knew he was a winner from the day he had interviewed him for the fellowship. "I think you're right, Arlene, it's time to get up and get going. No more moping."

"That's better," she said, "like last year. You started out depressed and wound up happy. Concentrate on the good things, Leo. Get these young men fired up to do great things." A peck on the cheek and she turned back under the covers. "Go to work," she ordered, but then her hand felt his sweat-drenched pillow, and she sat bolt upright, no longer playful.

"You've been having the nightmares again, haven't you?"

"Yes," he admitted.

"Why now?"

"I don't know."

"Yes, you do. I love you so much, but be honest with me, please."

"Takashi Yamamoto's coming to visit the dog lab and the clinical unit. I'm sorry, I should have told you."

"How long have you known?"

"A few weeks."

"It's for the medal, isn't it?"

"I'm not sure."

"Why else would he come now? It's that time again. That's why you're thinking of quitting. You don't want to be put on the spot."

Miller smiled. "Arlene you know too much about this business. I've trained you too well."

"True, and I also know when you're hurting," she said softly. "Which dream is it? The camp or the March?"

"The March. Lately it's always the March."

She kissed him gently on the forehead. "Take a shower and go to work. We'll talk again tonight."

He nodded. "Thanks," he said. "I love you."

CHAPTER

5

April, 1942

The sun was a bright red disc darting in and out of the stream of passing clouds. Its rays beat down unmercifully on the lines of American and Filipino POWs as they shuffled along the dusty highway that ran parallel to Manila Bay and led to points north. Whenever an exhausted POW collapsed to the ground, a Japanese guard repeatedly kicked and bayoneted him and then dragged the mangled body to the side of the road. It had been this way for the POWs for two days now, ever since their mass surrender all along the crumbling defense perimeter that separated their positions on the Bataan Peninsula from the South China Sea. Where—and when—their ordeal would end, none of the POWs knew or could even guess.

Picking his way carefully through the lines of men that had once formed the five companies of the 1st battalion of the 31st Infantry Regiment of the US Army, Major William Larsen, senior-most regimental battalion surgeon, looked for signs of imminent collapse among his "boys," especially the stragglers. He had seen too many of the weaker ones bayoneted already and was fearful that the number would only grow. Larsen's goal was to save as many as he could from the toll of the march simply by goading them to survive, since he had neither medicines, nor bandages, nor surgical instruments. When the Japanese guards signaled for one of their infrequent rest stops, and the prisoners quickly sprawled on the ground wherever space allowed, Larsen seized the opportunity to cheer up those soldiers who he thought needed his support the most. He spotted three of them who looked particularly shaky—two soldiers who seemed to be in their twenties and one not even that old.

"What's your name, son?" he said to the youngest as he squatted next to him.

"Leo Miller, sir." The youth was tall and lean with a hawk-like nose and not even a hint of stubble on his face. Too young to shave, Larsen thought.

"Where you from?"

"Haverhill, Massachusetts, sir."

"You going to be OK? You and your buddies look like shit."

"I dunno, I guess so. I feel better then I look." The youth laughed nervously. "Are any of us going to be OK?"

The doctor shrugged. "The younger you are, the better your chances. What are you—18, 19?"

"Eighteen, sir, I enlisted in '41, before Pearl Harbor. I wanted to fight the Nazis, and I figured we'd be in it soon enough. Instead I got shipped here, to the 31st. Some joke, huh?" he laughed. "No Nazis for me. Now I'm just one of the battling bastards of Bataan—you know the words, sir—no mama, no papa, no Uncle Sam." Larsen smiled. "Yep, I know the words."

Something about the way the medical officer carried himself seemed to cheer up the young soldier. "Think Corregidor can hold out till help arrives, sir?" Larsen knew no one was coming to save the little island in Manila Bay where MacArthur and his staff were holed up but he said maybe anyway.

Miller grew serious. "Will we ever make it home? he asked, with the bravado gone.

Larsen looked him squarely in the eye. "You'll make it," he said, trying to instill confidence in his tone, even if he didn't believe it. "But you've got to stay strong to take care of your buddies."

"Let me help you today," Miller said suddenly, "I'm better off if I can do something useful, anything."

"Sure why not, I can use help. Why not?" A Japanese guard cut off Larsen in mid-sentence, pulled him to his feet and yelled at him repeatedly, signaling with hand gestures for him to lead the others back on the trail. Larsen did as he was told.

Kicking up clouds of dust as they trekked north, Larsen and Miller took turns supporting weary soldiers until they were again able to walk on their own. As the afternoon turned into dusk, Larsen went up to the head of the line; Miller stayed in the middle.

Larsen went back from time to time to see how Miller was doing; surprisingly, the young soldier seemed invigorated by helping those who had fallen, whispering words of encouragement in their ears while keeping the mass of men moving. "You're a quick learner, with a good way about you," Larsen told him. "You could make a great doctor someday."

Miller beamed appreciatively and Larsen made his way forward to the head of the column. Miller's eyes followed his progress through the clouds of dust until the major disappeared from view.

CHAPTER

6

As O'Brien had predicted, the Japanese cardiologist arrived in College Station and was afforded VIP treatment by the staff of the Cardiology Section. Dr. Takashi Yamamoto was affable, elegant in dress, and, as a result of his primary school education and training at Johns Hopkins School of Medicine, spoke excellent English. He spent time observing all aspects of the section's activity but found the animal lab especially interesting, particularly Bergman's work. Bergman had become increasingly engrossed in one specific aspect of the experimental procedure, heretofore unresolved. What if the vessel could be plugged *internally* by some technique that did not require surgery? Then, the "heart attack" the animal experienced would be more closely related to one occurring in humans.

Bergman began working on an idea that had literally come to him in the middle of the night when he awoke at three a.m. and for some reason could not easily return to sleep. He had the presence of mind to write down his thoughts because, as he feared, when he awoke the next morning he could remember little of what he had conceived. Fortunately, his barely decipherable notes were on the bedside table where he left them.

What Bergman developed was a small plastic device that could be fastened to the end of a special catheter and inserted into the mouth of the coronary artery. The interior of the device was hollow so that blood could pass freely through it, but the inner surface absorbed fluid and would gradually swell, effectively blocking off the flow of blood within 24–48 hours. This would do away with the need for surgery, since the device could be introduced with the animal awake using only a local anesthetic agent.

With the active encouragement of Yamamoto, Bergman convinced O'Brien of the feasibility of his idea and without involving Sanderson, the three of them tested the method on several dogs using only local anesthesia. After a week of trial and error they proved to their own satisfaction that the plastic device indeed worked, but now they needed to convince Miller. O'Brien invited Miller to the lab to see a demonstration. Miller gave them all a benign smile saying softly, "This better be good," and stood off to the side to watch. An animal was taken from his cage, lightly medicated with a tranquilizer to keep him from squirming too much, and then strapped down on the operating table. Since the dog was awake and breathing normally, if somewhat slowly, there was no need to hook up a respirator and insert a breathing tube. Bergman inserted his device using a guide wire inside tubing that was inserted into the animal's leg artery and visualized on a monitor using an overhead x-ray machine. Advancing the tube catheter higher, he finally reached the mouth of the coronary arteries and placed the device. The whole procedure, to this point, had taken only three or four minutes.

Bergman then withdrew the guide wire and the catheter, put pressure on the thigh artery for five minutes to stop any bleeding, applied a dressing to the puncture site, and, several minutes later, the animal was allowed to run free again. He cavorted playfully for a few minutes and then was led into his cage where a bowl of chow awaited him.

O'Brien explained to Miller and Yamamoto that Bergman had gained the necessary experience with catheters and guide wires after only a few weeks of practice. Feeling quite pleased with himself, Bergman cleaned his instruments and prepared them for re-sterilization while waiting for some reaction from Miller. Miller remained impassive, as he had throughout the entire procedure, following Bergman's moves intently, but without comment. He made a few notes in a pad that he drew from the chest pocket of his white coat and then nodded to all of them and left. His face gave no hint of his thoughts.

"He wants to see the final result," O'Brien said, explaining Miller's apparent lack of enthusiasm while trying to cheer Bergman up at the same time. Bergman felt deflated but still hopeful. "He has to be very careful," Yamamoto said, to reassure him. "No use getting excited prematurely." Sure enough, the next day Miller was back, observing the animal in his cage. An electrocardiographic monitor had been attached to the dog and, from all indications, a coronary occlusion had not yet occurred. That afternoon, however, the electrocardiogram began to record abnormalities and the dog appeared to be uncomfortable.

Miller was informed and again returned. He studied the animal and the electrocardiographic tracing.

"The animal is having a heart attack but is still alive," he said. "Congratulations." He was beaming at both O'Brien and Bergman but said to Yamamoto, "Now they have to do it again, Takashi, to prove it wasn't a fluke." Yamamoto nodded in agreement. A similar experiment later that week again resulted in a non-fatal heart attack. Miller was delighted. Bergman had presented him with a better setting for studying some of the questions with which he was grappling. He invited Bergman to discuss this procedure at the section's next research conference. Two days later, Bergman used the blackboard in the conference room to diagram what he had done. The assembled group of Miller's staff and fellows seemed genuinely impressed. Afterwards, Adopolous slapped Bergman on the back in congratulations, Barnes whispered a "well done," and Douglas stared at Bergman in awe. Miller said little, but instead studied the reactions of the others. He huddled with O'Brien and Yamamoto before leaving, a big smile on his face.

The next day, O'Brien told Bergman that Miller was indeed quite impressed with the work and wanted him to prepare a summary of it for submission as a paper to be considered for presentation at the next National Cardiology Society meeting in the winter. With Miller's seal of approval, O'Brien's attitude toward Bergman had warmed considerably—no more "fucking asshole" remarks.

At the same time, Sanderson grew noticeably cooler and was rude to him the few times they did interact. "Watch where you're putting your stuff, you clumsy oaf! That coffee cup is right on top of my data pages!"

Bergman was sure that Sanderson felt he had upstaged him and didn't like it. Still, Bergman couldn't let that distract him. He had to prepare a 250-word summary of the experiments and only had a week to do it before the submission deadline.

After struggling through several drafts, with no prior experience in abstract writing, and with the deadline for submission now only several days away, Bergman approached Yamamoto for help, and the distinguished visitor was glad to assist him. "I'm going back to Tokyo next week and seeing your experiments up close was one of the highlights of my visit."

"Do you do this often, visit a colleague's institution for a short stay?"

"Normally not this long." Yamamoto smiled. "Let's just say it's part of my job as President of the Japanese Medical Society. I think it will all be more understandable in a month or so."

"Sounds mysterious."

"Yes, a little. But now let's get back to this paper so that Professor Miller is pleased with it."

Bergman finally gave what he thought was a presentable abstract to Miller's secretary. Within several hours, she called him back to inform him that Miller wanted to go over it with him, but, because he had a full schedule of appointments during the day and because of the deadline, could Bergman meet with him at his home in the evening? Bergman agreed, and the secretary gave him directions.

CHAPTER

7

August 1942

Throughout the American POW camp, the soldiers were dying. There was nothing Larsen and Miller or any of the other makeshift medical personnel they relied upon could do about it. A combination of starvation and disease took their daily toll, but there were also those who died from the lingering effects of battle wounds, or injuries suffered on the march up the Bataan peninsula, or later from the beatings by Japanese guards in the camp. The dead were buried in shallow graves on the outskirts of the camp, just beyond the wire fences. Sometimes the soldiers died slowly and in agony (there was no morphine), sometimes quickly in a fit of delirium. Today's death was one of the latter. "Betty where are you?" the grizzled sergeant moaned, his head cradled in Larsen's hands while Miller gently poured tepid water into his parched throat. "God damn it, I need you now, Betty, now."

"His temperature must be 102 or 103 degrees at least," Larsen whispered to Miller. "Can you come up with any aspirin so we can bring the fever down?" He looked around the dilapidated shack they were using as an infirmary in disgust. "Maybe we can make him more comfortable before . . ." He nodded silently at the sergeant and Miller understood.

"I got some from the Filipino women from Cabanatuan who comes in to clean the Jap officer quarters," Miller said. "They smuggled in plenty this time. How many you need?"

"Just two, that's all, to help break the fever."

The aspirin soon took effect. The sergeant began sweating profusely, his temperature came down, and he briefly became lucid again.

"Where am I doc? Am I in heaven yet?" He looked up at the two of them with wide, frightened eyes.

"No, sarge, you're still in hell."

"Won't be long, doc. They beat the crap out of me just for trying to get a little more rice. Christ, I hate all these fucking Japs." He closed his eyes while Miller ran a wet rag across his forehead.

"Do you hate all the Japs, Leo?" Larsen said, turning to Miller.

The young man didn't hesitate. "You bet I do."

"Will you still hate them ... later, if there is a later?"

"I can never forget the march, I can't. One of my buddies was bayoneted to death, and the other one is dying of malaria. I won't forget the march *or* this camp—if I ever get out of here ... , " Miller's voice trailed off.

"I told you, you're young and strong, you'll make it if anyone does. But I don't want you to be a hater. Do you understand me?"

"No. No, I don't," Miller replied with puzzlement. "How can I forget?"

"Don't forget. Never forget, just don't hate them all," Larsen said wearily. "Don't you believe in God?"

"I don't listen to the chaplains anymore."

"I still do," Larsen said, "For whatever the hell the reason, I still do."

"The sergeant's sleeping," Miller said. "Did God do that? Should we be thankful for small miracles, Major?"

"Exactly," Larsen said, wearily, and patted Miller softly on the head, while they waited quietly for the sergeant to die.

CHAPTER

8

The Millers ate dinner in silence until Leo turned to his wife and smiled proudly.

"My hunch about young Bergman seems to be working out. He's doing really good work in the dog lab. Really good work. He's coming over later to work on an abstract."

"O'Brien likes him?"

"As much as he can like anybody."

"Hey, you lay off O'Brien," she said, laughing.

"I'm the boss so I'm allowed to poke fun at his dour personality."

"But only if the lab is humming along okay, right?"

"Exactly. And it's doing quite well. Sanderson's terrific. Best worker we've ever had here, churns out experiments like crazy. So everything's great, just in time for Takashi Yamamoto's visit."

His wife put down her knife and fork. "When are you going to talk to him about the prize?" Her tone was no longer light.

"I decided not to," Miller said, squirming uneasily. "I don't know how to bring it up without appearing presumptuous."

"But you don't want to put him in an uncomfortable position with his colleagues in Tokyo, much less the Japanese government. You like Takashi, why not just sit down and explain your feelings about the Emperor. I'm sure he'd understand, and it could save you a lot of embarrassment. Maybe the goddamn nightmares would go away. Last night you were moaning in your sleep again. Really, Leo, think about talking to him."

"Arlene, I don't want to make a fool of him, but I feel silly bringing up the prize without even knowing they're planning to give it to me."

His wife shook her head. "I think you're wrong, Leo. Now let's finish dinner before Bergman arrives."

CHAPTER

9

In the early part of the evening, while it was still light, Bergman drove to Miller's home in a suburb north of the city. Nearly all of the houses were offset from the street by spacious, well-manicured lawns. Bergman could see it was an affluent area, but not overly ostentatious. The Millers lived in a white frame house with black shutters bracketing the windows, surrounded by a dense hedge. Neatly arranged flower beds filled with masses of impatiens bordered the front steps. Dressed as he had been at the hospital, Miller answered the door with an effusive welcome and escorted Bergman into a large den that opened onto a screened porch.

"Come on in. Just finished dinner."

Bergman noticed again what a large man he was. With his thick hair askew, it was like following a grizzly into his favorite lair.

The night was cool for early August, but not uncomfortably so, and an endless chorus of crickets bombarded the pair as they sat in overstuffed leather chairs in the softly lit room. From somewhere in the background, baroque music filtered through the night. It was one of the Brandenburg concertos, Miller explained, and they chatted a bit about music. "With some exceptions, it seems my interest stopped at the turn of the eighteenth century," Miller explained. After some more small talk, he shifted to a more personal note.

"Paul, I've been very impressed with your work. Charlie O'Brien speaks very highly of you, and he's usually a good judge of what it takes to be successful in cardiology research."

"I appreciate that, sir."

"This is not the military so no more of that sir stuff. Please!"

He opened his collar, loosened his tie, and again, as he did so often, pushed back the hair from his forehead.

"You're a quiet sort of fellow, but you're steady, and you see to it that what needs to be done gets done. O'Brien has told me how you persevered despite his initial misgivings about the feasibility of your project. More than anything else, I appreciate someone like that, someone who sets his sights on a goal and goes after it. Sanderson's like that, and he's been very successful." Miller stretched his legs before him and carefully rubbed his chin. It was a pleasant atmosphere—plush leather chairs, the pulsating baroque music; even the sound of the crickets was restful. "You know the importance of my work," Miller continued, "but what you may or may not know is that others are also working on the same project."

"I wasn't aware of that," Bergman said.

"It doesn't matter. No one's really gotten a good handle on the technique of inducing the initial insult in a non-traumatic, reproducible manner. Bernstein at Harvard and Connolly at Columbia would give their eye teeth for that little device you thought up."

"Maybe it would be better *not* to report on the device for the time being," Bergman offered. "That would give us a little lead time to do more with it before others could produce their own. There's nothing really that esoteric about it."

"That occurred to me," Miller said after a while, "but I'm a bit surprised you thought of it. That's a bit precocious for a trainee."

Bergman reddened slightly.

"In any event, the NCS, the National Cardiac Society, has a meeting in five months and by that time we'll have enough data in the can, so to speak, that we'll not have to worry about the others catching up, at least for the time being. Remember, Paul, the most important thing is to eventually share these advances with our colleagues." He looked Bergman squarely in the eye. "Advancing medical science is the main objective of all experimentation, so that eventually patients can be benefited. Personal recognition is a minor aspect and will come later."

The tone of his remark caused Bergman to redden even more. He felt ashamed to have even brought up the subject, albeit indirectly, of personal "gain." "Let's get down to business," Miller said. "Move your chair closer to mine. If we get this abstract in decent shape, I see no reason why you won't be making your first important presentation at the NCS meeting in New York. Takashi told me he helped a bit, so it shouldn't be that difficult for us to finish up. He's a good man, Dr. Yamamoto, but I just wish ...." He stopped in mid-sentence, as if uncomfortable about continuing.

For the next hour, they went over the wording of the abstract while one Brandenburg concerto followed another until finally the compact disc came to its end. Miller had little difficulty in trimming the report to the prescribed word limit and, by changing a phrase here and there and inserting certain key words, he made the meaning much clearer. He thought Bergman's title was too dull and substituted one of his own, one that was more provocative ("Do You Always Have to Open the Chest to Create an Experimental Coronary Occlusion?") and would catch the eye of the reviewer who might have to review some fifty of these as part of the selection process. Satisfied at last, Miller replaced the Bach with Corelli's trumpet concerto, lit a pipe, and puffed away while the strident tones of the brass now filled the night air.

He offered Bergman a glass of port, his favorite after-dinner drink, and they both sipped their liqueurs in silence. Finally, Miller stood and stretched. "You're going to have another few weeks in the dog lab before you start your next clinical rotation, but if you still feel you need additional time there, come in on nights and weekends whenever possible, because I think this project deserves the highest priority. O'Brien and Sanderson will help you. They're great workers. Nothing should interfere with this project's completion, and I'm confident a half-dozen more completely instrumented animals will do it," he said, then smiled. "You're going to be the first author—the main author—on a fine abstract. Sanderson will be second, O'Brien third, and I think I've been helpful enough tonight to warrant the last place, which is usually an honorary position for the head of the division whether they earn it or not. Still, I feel strongly that all secondary authors should contribute something, since having your name on an abstract or article means you're responsible for its contents. You know, seeing you getting excited about this reminds me of my own start in the lab. Long, long, hours, no question about it. I sometimes wonder if it would have been better if I had just gone into practice and become a family doctor working out there in those lovely hills. In a few weeks, the leaves will be turning in a way that you've never seen in New York. New England at its best, no question about it. Practicing in the countryside and watching the change of seasons wouldn't have been bad at all." He puffed at his pipe and gazed a bit wistfully out to the porch where the sound of the crickets was still loud and where, in the distance, though they couldn't see them in the darkness, were all those hills he had just fantasized about.

"Sorry, but I can't agree with you," Bergman said, as respectfully as possible. "I just can't see a man of your many talents in medicine being just a country doctor. You'd miss all the stimulation of the academic environment."

"Ah, I see you've already been bitten by the same bug that got me, way back when. Better watch out, it can be a fatal disease." He chuckled through the pipe smoke. "You'll find out it's not really all stimulation and excitement. There's too much administrative work, too many personality conflicts to sort out among the staff, salary raises for secretaries to negotiate, and so forth. And then there's the politics of it. So much politics. And I've made my enemies—people I've criticized in editorials, in meetings. I'm known as a hard critic, but I think I'm fair. Even so, some people take it all very badly. Ed Smith in Chicago hardly even speaks to me anymore. Maybe you remember his group's paper last year in the *American Cardiology Journal*? I ripped it to pieces in a letter to the editor, and why not, it was junk." His face grew more animated now, and he put down his port; the pipe waved back and forth in his hand. "Of course, I didn't say it was junk in the letter; I wouldn't do that; just said it was shaky science, full of flaws."

"If it was that bad, how did it get past the reviewers?"

"Ha, you've still got a lot to learn, I can see that. The editor or one of his associates decides which reviewers to send it to. If it's sent to one of Smith's pals—and there's a regular old-boy network, worse than the State Department—then they handle it with kid gloves. Well, not always, of course," he qualified himself, "but often. To tell the truth, Ed Smith's an asshole and always has been. Excuse the language."

"You didn't always think so poorly of him," a woman's voice said, and Bergman turned in surprise. An attractive, middle-aged blonde had entered the room.

"You and Ed Smith were once good friends."

Bergman saw that she carried a highball glass in her hand.

Miller rose hastily. "Arlene, this is Paul Bergman; Paul, my wife Arlene."

Arlene smiled at Bergman politely and sat down on the leather couch opposite their easy chairs. "Would you like me to freshen your drink, dear?" Miller asked solicitously.

"No thanks, Leo. You know, it's funny, how you feel about Ed Smith. I remember when he and Lucy and the two of us were a foursome back in those years of training in Boston."

"That was long time ago," Miller said, forcing a smile, "before Paul even knew what a stethoscope was." His wife now directed her gaze toward the younger man, crossing her long legs in front of her. Her face was thin, poised, her eyes a clear blue. "Where are you from?"

"New York."

"How do you like our little city?"

"It's not that little," Bergman protested.

"Little compared to New York," she insisted. "Are you married?"

"No."

Miller cleared his throat. "Paul has just started in the dog lab, dear."

His wife scowled." Ah yes. Leo's dungeon, as O'Brien calls it. Once you get involved in one of O'Brien's experiments down there, you won't have much time for anything else. It's a good thing you're not married; wives are very demanding. Which reminds me, Leo, Helen Zimmerman tells me you've gotten involved in a little campus controversy that has all my friends upset."

"Well, Arlene I don't want to upset you or your friends, but I had to chair a faculty senate committee that was looking into one of the sociology professors who was making statements that women are genetically inferior to men when it comes to math and physics."

"That's ridiculous."

"Of course it is, but he shouldn't be fired just because he thinks that way. Or so I convinced my committee."

His wife's face dropped. "I should have known it was true that you were involved. I'll have to apologize to Helen." She shook her head in disgust.

"Free speech, nothing more, nothing less; the cornerstone of a university. No matter how unpleasant the beliefs—short of a call to violence—they must be allowed."

Arlene shook her head and excused herself.

"Free speech ought to be the concern of all of us," Miller said after she left. "I guess I'm just an old-fashioned libertarian and proud of it. Now go home, Paul, and get some sleep. We may still want to tune-up that abstract in the morning. And don't worry about the women's groups. In a short time, they'll forget all about this business. You'll see. Tomorrow, let's find out what Takashi thinks about the new version of the abstract."

"Excuse me Dr. Miller, I really enjoyed interacting with Dr. Yamamoto, but I got the feeling earlier that you had some reservations about him ..."

Miller shook his head. "No, no, no. Nothing like that. I admire Takashi tremendously. He's had to overcome a lot of resentment in the US because his uncle was Admiral Yamamoto, who orchestrated the Pearl Harbor attack. Not a lot of people know that, but some of those who do have strong feelings about it. I don't because it had nothing to do with him, and, believe me, I have stronger feelings than most for a variety of reasons—but that's neither here nor there. I'm just a little concerned that his visit to us in his official capacity could cause some problems." Bergman was truly puzzled, but said nothing. "Look, these problems may never come to pass, but if they do I'll share them with you. It's sort of a personal issue so I'd just as soon stop the conversation here. Never should have started it in the first place." He frowned and Bergman quickly got up to leave, sorry he had brought the matter up.

On the way back to campus, he forgot about Yamamoto and thought again about the abstract—his abstract, his first abstract—going over it again and again in his mind. He felt as though it was a part of him now, an offspring. It was a good feeling. Miller was right. He had been bitten by the bug.

CHAPTER

10

When October arrived and the foliage became as brilliant as Miller had predicted, Bergman started the clinical-service rotation, which meant he was involved in the care of patients admitted to the hospital. Although his days were too busy for anything but patient-related matters, he did manage to spend several nights and weekends in the animal lab completing an additional series of experiments with his occluding device. There was, now, more than enough data to support the initial impression that had been reported in the abstract. He soon learned that the abstract had been accepted for presentation, receiving one of the highest grades in its category. Miller was extremely pleased at this news and urged Bergman to prepare a paper for submission to a medical journal.

Soon after, Bergman was surprised to be called into Wentworth's office. He had never been alone with the Chairman of the Department of Medicine since his arrival in July. Wentworth was all smiles as he led him to a comfortable seat near his desk. Sitting down himself, he said, "I was extremely pleased to hear that you've already dived into an exciting research project and got an abstract accepted for presentation. But I just wanted to offer you a bit of advice about dealing with some of Leo Miller's staff, especially Dr. O'Brien. That man is a vulgar ruffian, no other way to say it. I don't know why Leo puts up with him."

"I wasn't aware..."

"No, of course not. I didn't think you would be. The truth of the matter is that keeping O'Brien around sullies the school's reputation. I've said that to Leo many, many times but he ignores me. Just beware of becoming too closely entangled with O'Brien."

Bergman was stunned. What had O'Brien specifically done to earn him such enmity from the Chair of Medicine and at the same time such loyalty from the Chief of Cardiology?

"If you observe things that distress or upset you with the cardiology program don't hesitate to come directly to me," Wentworth concluded. "I will protect your confidence. Thanks again for coming in today."

With that, Bergman was dismissed, the reason for his visit still unclear in his mind. Later that night he told Jennifer Steiner of his good fortune—and the strange visit to Wentworth that followed. It was only their second date, but he found it was surprisingly easy to talk to her about things that were on his mind. Their first date had been a quick dinner sandwiched into his on-call schedule, but her easy manner and engaging laughter had whetted his appetite for spending more time with her. Tonight he had the time to take her to a real restaurant.

"You're a psychologist. Maybe you can help figure out what Wentworth had in mind," he said, while cutting through his leg of lamb.

She poked at her roast chicken before answering. "Sounds like he was trying to cause a rift between you and O'Brien . . . to embarrass Miller, possibly?"

"I don't know. Wentworth knows I'm Miller's fellow, so of course I'm going to be loyal to Miller even if I start to have doubts about O'Brien."

"Not too subtle, was he?"

"No, not at all. Not exactly what I expected from someone in his position. It's puzzling."

"Do you like O'Brien?"

"Like is not the right word. He's strange, but okay, I guess. Sanderson's a piece of work, too, but Miller's crazy about him."

"Sanderson gives me the creeps," Jennifer said, then returned to her chicken.

"You know you are positively beautiful when you eat chicken," Bergman said, ending all talk of the dog lab.

"Why Dr. Bergman, I thought you'd never notice!"

After he dropped her off at her apartment, he told himself he had never met anyone as wonderful as Jennifer Steiner. I'm falling in love with her, he thought. It was a little scary, considering he hardly knew her, but just a little.

CHAPTER

11

Now that Bergman was on the clinical service, he saw Miller on almost a daily basis. Many of the patients admitted to the cardiology service of the hospital for diagnosis and/or treatment had come there specifically to be under Miller's care; as the cardiology fellow, Bergman acted as Miller's subaltern in communicating his wishes to the interns and residents. Miller presented yet another side of his personality when he was with his patients. He was extremely affable and would often chat with them for, what seemed to Bergman, inordinately long periods of time. He listened sympathetically while they told him of their chest pain, or their shortness of breath, their irregular heartbeats, or whatever they complained of. Fear of dying was a subject that he had to deal with continually, and he handled the issue skillfully.

As Bergman observed Miller on his rounds, he came to agree with Miller's comment that he probably would have made a good country doctor. But, he reminded himself at those moments of how much Miller's work with heart disease could benefit so many thousands of patients; he had much more to offer than merely compassion, good diagnostic acumen, and carefully planned therapeutic regimens. He had the resources of his research laboratories, the enthusiasm of bright associates and fellows, and his own insights, all of which could well revolutionize how patients with heart disease were treated. In that sense, he clearly would be wasting his potential as a country doctor or, for that matter, in any setting very different from the present one.

Somewhere in this stage of their relationship, Miller became the bigger-than-life icon that Bergman had wanted him to be and expected him to be since the day that he had first applied to his fellowship program. While Bergman was on the clinical service, he did whatever was necessary to keep Miller satisfied: made sure that the patients' medical histories were presented to him as concisely as possible, which was the way he preferred it, that all laboratory test results were available as soon as possible (often the same day they were done), that orders for changes in medication were quickly carried out by the nurses, etc. In turn, Miller seemed to genuinely appreciate Bergman's extra effort and, despite his occasional brusqueness, he found himself developing a real fondness for Miller. When Adopolous and Bergman chatted on Friday afternoon in the hospital auditorium before the start of one of the weekly clinical conferences, Adopolous seemed amazed at how well Bergman was getting on with Miller.

"He still scares the hell out of me," Adopolous said. "Ever since my run-in with him that first day, he hardly says a word to me. But I heard I'm not the only one he cold-shoulders. There are a lot of first-rate people at the hospital and medical school that can't stand him. And the women's groups at the university are mad as hell at him."

"I have no complaints," Bergman said, and repeated what Miller had told him about the sociology professor. "The women's groups will get over it. Free speech is important in a university."

Adopolous laughed. "Don't lecture me with that crap. Miller was just on an ego trip, that's all. Hell, he's worse than O'Brien and O'Brien's a real nut," Adopolous continued. He had just started in the animal lab and, being somewhat clumsy, was feeling the full force of O'Brien's sporadic rages. "But at least with Crazy Charlie you always know what to expect; you don't hope to walk into the lab and find him transformed because you know it's not possible. With Miller it's different. Because he is who he is, you always hope he'll suddenly turn into a nice guy like Rogers. Why can't he be more like Rogers?"

Rogers was the chief clinical assistant to Miller and, like Wentworth, was a native of the state with patrician roots. "Douglas and Barnes like Rogers a lot, too. Maybe because he doesn't have Miller's great aspiration, he treats us like real people, not like soldiers always on parade. I think Miller would step on his own mother if she got in the way of his research. I know it's a rotten thing to say, but the longer I'm here the more I believe it, and I'm not the only one."

The disappointment in his tone was disheartening to Bergman because he liked Adopolous and he liked Miller. But Bergman understood his feelings. As if to emphasize Adopolous' criticisms, Miller castigated Barnes unmercifully during the conference for a particularly sloppy and long-winded presentation. Afterwards, on rounds, Miller spoke to Bergman about it.

"Don't ever present a case like Barnes did today. It sets an awful example for the medical students and house staff and reflects poorly on the whole cardiology program. I make a point of selecting what I feel are outstanding fellowship applicants from all over the country to show the drawing power of this hospital, and then when one of them does a poor job it makes all my efforts worthless. Furthermore, case presentations are a particular bugaboo of Wentworth's. He insists on postcard-pretty presentations, and it's one of the few things that I can see to it he gets. There's certainly not much else I can do to please him."

Again, there was the rancor in his tone when discussing his boss—the same rancor Bergman had heard in his chat with Wentworth—though Bergman still could not understand why. Miller's almost bearish appearance was in contrast to the extremely tall, thin, and fine-featured Wentworth as if to further highlight their differences.

"Rounds this afternoon are going to be quick," Miller continued. "I'm taking my wife up to our lake cottage for the weekend. We need a little time to ourselves. I'm afraid with all the time I spend at the hospital, she sometimes feels neglected." Then, quickly changing the subject, which Bergman felt he had brought up because of the near-scene at his house the night they were going over the abstract, he asked which patients Bergman was going to show him that afternoon.

"We have three patients in the Special Intensive Care Unit that you should look in on before you leave. The rest of your patients are all stable, and I can see them later."

"Three sounds fine."

Their pace quickened as they neared the SIRU, as it was more commonly called. This was Miller's pride and joy. Financed entirely out of federal and private grants, it was the hub of his clinical research. Whatever breakthroughs were made in the animal laboratory would ultimately have to undergo their most severe test in humans housed on that unit. Every patient admitted to the SIRU agreed to participate in one or another of the research protocols in which Miller's group was involved. They did so willingly, so commanding was his reputation as a leader in medical science and as a healer of those patients on whom other physicians had given up.

Turning off the main corridor into a short hallway, the doors ahead of them swung open automatically, and they entered the restricted domain of the SIRU. Essentially, it was one very large room with an open central area and a periphery, coming off the central core like the spokes of a wheel, divided into several patient cubicles and various related rooms. The core, monitored by an experienced nurse, contained an electronic console with screens showing the electrocardiograms, heart rates, etc. of all patients currently on the unit.

The last of the three patients was the most difficult one. Miller's disposition turned gloomy as Bergman pointed to cubicle number three. He knew what to expect. This was Mrs. Wilson's cubicle. The unfortunate woman had come over a thousand miles to be under his care, but there was nothing he could do for her. She lay dying a slow and predictable death, her heart rocked by spasms of irregular heartbeats that set the chambers to beating erratically and out of sequence, and then eased off on their own or through drugs—only to return again hours later. There was no surgical cure. Her coronary arteries were spotted throughout with obstructions that were made worse by the intermittent spasms, and her heart muscle was scarred severely from previous heart attacks. She had been in the SIRU for over two weeks. Bergman briefly summed up her situation and added that there was nothing new to report. She had another episode that day, much like all the others, with marked irregularities of the heart beat. These episodes were becoming more difficult to control; even the experimental newly implanted defibrillator was unable to stop all the spasms, and they were running out of drugs to try. Miller rocked back and forth on his heels, his head bowed, and one hand covering his forehead. It was as if he were going into a trance, and when Bergman had finished his summary, none of them dared break the spell. They knew that when he was ready, he would speak.

"If only I could do something," he said in a very somber voice. "My God, this is the key to it all. If we could help Mrs. Wilson, then we'd really be on top of it, at last we'd be on top of it. But how to find the answer? I tell you, honestly, I don't know."

Behind the folding glass doors of her cubicle, she stared out at the team, waxen and frightened, surrounded by the monitor screens depicting her heart rhythm in greenish waves. But this was no animal stretched out on an operating table. There was no way that they could isolate the heart, try this remedy first and then that one, and if all failed, simply let the heart stop, and begin the experiment all over on a new dog. This was a human being who was suffering, with loved ones who cared, with a life she was not yet ready to give up.

Miller mused as he prepared to enter her cubicle, "What a shame. We've got to find a way to get into the human heart, to unravel its mysteries, or else we're all failures. Do you understand what I'm saying?" Now he was looking at Bergman. "Do you see what drives me to unlock that door and to find the Holy Grail with its tiny seed of wisdom? That's the noblest cause of all that will yield the greatest glory of all because it will do the greatest good of all. Nothing else matters, nothing." He strode by them then into the room and sat down by her side, stroked her hand, consoled her. Her drooping eyes lit up at his presence. Despite all the flashing lights and monitor screens about him, it was still the simple act of compassion, the human contact that mattered now. He personified the magic and mystery of the physician, and he knew it. He used this power to calm the patient. She grew more relaxed; her eyes shone more brightly, her lips stopped shaking. Spirit again seemed to flow through her tired body.

"You will not die," he was telling her ever so softly and gently. "I will not let you." And she nodded, with complete faith in him as if he were a Hindu mystic, African witch doctor, and carnival faith healer all rolled into one. What did it matter if his words were untruths, he would say later to the team. She needed to believe him for the time when the agony of another spasm would rack her heart. Would she renounce him then? No, she would still have faith, because she knew he would be trying in some mystical way to fight the forces of death that assaulted her unrelentingly.

Miller came out of the cubicle, his face angry. Ignoring the others for the moment, he put his arm around Bergman. "Paul, this is the quest, nothing else matters. This is what my life's work is all about. We've got to learn all we can, and that's why your invention is so helpful. When we learn all we can, we must attack and attack until we have licked it and no one need fear this damned thing again."

"What about one of the new experimental drugs? O'Brien's been working on several."

"Not yet, not yet. To use them properly, we must know what they do, and we still don't know. And the side effects are atrocious. Remember the first rule of medicine. Do no harm. We don't want to kill this lady trying to save her. No, we just have to admit that we don't know; that we don't have the answer—not now anyway." Still obviously upset, he walked off the unit without good-byes to the staff, the automatic doors opening and then shutting behind him.

"Whew!" said the resident, "what an experience. I haven't seen him like this for quite a while."

Even the nurses, who had seen him on more rounds than any of them, were impressed. It was Leo Miller at his best: the physician, the scientist, the philosopher, the preacher.

That night, Mrs. Wilson had a particularly violent attack. The erratic heartbeat that Miller was so obsessed with became completely unresponsive to any of the drugs that were tried. Even electrical countershocks did not work. In the early hours of the morning, the exhausted heart could no longer supply itself with enough oxygenated blood and at last stopped completely. They had done what they could, but it was not enough. The peace of death had claimed her. Bergman called the woman's husband to tell him the sad news. He had prepared him for this ever since they realized the precariousness of her condition. But still, the husband was grief-stricken.

It was four a.m.; Bergman knew Miller was asleep at his lakeside cottage, and he debated whether to disturb him or wait until morning. He had the feeling that Miller would want to know immediately, and he was right.

"You know, Paul, every time I lose one of these patients, I think I lose a little of myself," he said wearily. "It's a rotten feeling."

"I'm sorry to start your weekend like this."

"But that's my life, Paul—and yours too, now—so the sooner one gets used to it the better. You get some sleep and don't worry about my weekends. The leaves are beautiful. For me, there's always solace in that. Go get some sleep."

Bergman tried but tossed and turned until dawn; then he called Jennifer.

"Sorry," he whispered, "but I had a rough night, and I missed you."

"Bergman, this must be getting serious," she whispered back, "because I missed you too and I didn't even have a rough day."

"You are the most exciting, the most scrumptious woman I've ever known."

"Scrumptious? I like that a lot. But it's five o'clock, so right now I'm going back to sleep. See you tonight?"

"You bet." Bergman set his alarm for seven a.m. and sunk his head into the pillow.

CHAPTER

12

There were several other patients like Mrs. Wilson admitted to the hospital during the fall and winter of 1989, the first year of Bergman's fellowship—some the cardiac team could save, some they couldn't. Miller's team had developed a tremendous expertise in treating complications of heart attacks, but the solution to the problem of severely erratic heart rhythms continued to elude them. They did not know how to identify those individuals whose course would be complicated by potentially fatal conditions. To identify the individuals beforehand would mean that sooner or later, with any luck at all, the team could devise ways to "pre-treat" them and prevent what very well might be cardiac catastrophe. This problem had become an obsession to Miller, as he readily admitted, and he devoted most of his waking hours to its resolution, either supervising O'Brien's activities in the animal laboratory or caring—with the help of Rogers—for those patients admitted to the hospital. But even the busiest of services (as theirs certainly was) needed its periods of relaxation. At Christmas time, the Millers threw an annual party for the staff and fellows and their wives and girlfriends. This gave Bergman the unusual opportunity of viewing the whole cardiology section on display in an informal setting.

Seeing the Miller home in the winter was a different experience altogether for Bergman, compared to his initial visit. Except for the evergreens, the trees were completely bare. The flowers were replaced by a mantle of white from a several-day-old snowfall that would be continually added to if past winters were a guideline and probably would remain on the ground until early April.

Bergman parked behind a line of earlier arrivals and made his way gingerly across the frozen walk, his breath hanging before him in the frigid air. One of the women hired to help with the party answered the door and took his coat. He went into the large den, which was rapidly filling with people. Bergman recognized quite a few of the staff doctors, but didn't know one wife from another. Glancing around the room, he soon spied the familiar faces of his colleagues. When Adopolous saw him, he elbowed his way through the partygoers with an extra cup of eggnog. He was beaming, an unusual sight lately.

"Why so happy?" Bergman asked.

"Probably too much to drink, the holiday season, who knows, who cares? Christ, I can't stay mad at the world this time of the year."

"Where's your wife?"

"She's tucked in a corner somewhere with Joan Barnes comparing notes on diaper brands. That's a mess you bachelors don't have to contend with. But where's Jennifer, the gal you're always talking about?"

"In Boston with her parents. Back Monday."

They stood and watched the passing scene, occasionally sampling the eggnog that was laced generously with superb rum. The other two first-year fellows, Douglas and Barnes, stopped by for a moment, and the four compared notes on the year to date. Douglas was enjoying himself and had lived in Massachusetts so long he hardly missed his native Atlanta, but Barnes and his wife had decided they did not like New England winters. And this one was only half over! Barnes' wife exclaimed to anyone who would listen about the perennial sunshine of southern California. She was fighting off one cold after another and was afraid of catching the flu next. After Douglas and Barnes had drifted off, Sanderson and one of the cardiac surgical fellows trooped by, busily planning a series of excursions during the cardiology meetings in New York, now just a month off. Between theater and basketball games, they had managed to fill every available night, much to the delight of the wives and girlfriends who had been invited to join them.

In addition to the fellows, the staff members were there in force; Rogers and O'Brien and their wives, and Goldberg and Donovan, who directed the intensive care unit and cardiac catheterization laboratories, respectively. Both were divorced, but they had little else in common and were constantly squabbling. The cardiac surgeons were present, led by Barker, their chief. There were also several other cardiologists who were not part of Miller's group, but who enjoyed part-time status on the faculty.

Boisterous laughter filled the room. Everyone seemed to be in a good mood and Goldberg and Donovan had momentarily put their feuding aside. As Adopolous said, it was probably the effect of the holiday season. Even the entrance of the distinguished Chief of Medicine, Harrison Wentworth, was not accompanied by the customary scowl from Miller. Instead, he shook Wentworth's hand warmly, gave Wentworth's wife an affectionate peck on the cheek, and he and Arlene Miller engaged them in light conversation for several minutes. That neither couple bore especially friendly feelings toward the other—not a secret by any means—was carefully hidden in an elaborate show of good manners against the background of a blazing fire, the constant clink of glasses and eggnog cups, and the tones of one or another baroque concerto that emanated from the stereo speakers.

"Look, maybe I'm just a dumb farm boy," Adopolous said to Bergman after viewing the Wentworths and Millers engrossed in one of Miller's humorous stories, "but I am very impressed by how these—these hypocrites, that's the only word—play this game so well. I could never pull it off. Neither could my wife. I can't see us putting aside feeling that strong even for an occasion like this."

"Gus, you're wrong; of course you could. I bet you do it at your family reunions. You do it when you see old college chums that you really couldn't stand. We all do it. Leo has to do it, so he does it, and from what I gather about Wentworth, he's an old hand at this, sort of comes in his bloodlines. Just be thankful that in the final analysis they're human after all and that they can act like civilized beings for a few minutes, even if they do have their petty jealousies like everyone else."

"Why are you so sure they're petty?"
"What do you know that I don't?"
"I hear things."
"Like what?"
Adopolous shrugged. "Some things you're better off not knowing about."

"Cut that crap. I like you too much to think you'd hide something from me and protest it's for my own good."

Bergman's tone was a hurt one, and Adopolous recognized it as such. The two of them had hit it off well. Not that they didn't like Douglas and Barnes, or the second-year fellows, for that matter; it was just that Bergman had taken a special liking to this sleepy-eyed buckeye (he subsequently learned after that first day in July he *always* looked tired), and Adopolous had reciprocated. As a result, Bergman couldn't see him withholding something from him that he might be interested in hearing.

Adopolous apologized, "you're right," he said. "I'm being pigheaded."

"Then, let's hear it."

Adopolous looked uncomfortable, but he blurted it out anyway. "It has to do with Arlene Miller and Charlie O'Brien. At one of the Wentworths' holiday parties a few years back—ten, maybe, I'm not sure—O'Brien got piss-headed drunk and vomited repeatedly on their Persian carpets. Acted obnoxious, before finally passing out. Wentworth wanted him fired, but Arlene convinced Leo to send O'Brien to rehab instead. This infuriated Wentworth even more, since he had dated Arlene before Leo came along and still considered her a friend."

"But those things were in the past," Bergman argued.

"True," Adopolous said, "but apparently Wentworth hasn't forgotten. Hard to believe, something as long ago as that could bother our boss."

He was right, of course, Bergman agreed, yet the thought added a sour note to the otherwise festive occasion. They sipped some more eggnog while the party wound down.

The Wentworths soon departed for another similar gathering at another faculty member's house, stopping first to wish each of the doctors a happy New Year. As always, Harrison Wentworth was smooth and professional in his manner.

Bergman had difficulty generating any real animosity toward him, even after his own meeting with him, or what Adopolous had told him. But if Miller had a problem with him ...; it was a disquieting thought. One by one, the other couples and the few single guests drifted out. Miller and his wife stood at the door with their arms around one another and wished all well. It was good for the fellows to see him in such a jovial mood. Perhaps those weekends by the lake had given him peace of mind. Bergman hoped so.

CHAPTER

13

The aura of the holiday season persisted through the New Year and into the preparation for the cardiology meetings. It was because of these meetings that, in mid-January, Bergman found himself back in New York City, ensconced in a hotel on the west side of Manhattan. The building was enormous, even by New York standards. Because of its excellent function rooms, it served as the headquarters hotel for the yearly National Cardiology Society meeting. The temperature was several degrees warmer in Manhattan than in New England, and Bergman eagerly roamed around town, renewing his acquaintance with the city as well as spending time with his parents.

As Miller had prophesied, the converted hotel ballroom was packed for the first morning session. The scientific selection committee had grouped together a series of particularly interesting abstracts dealing with experimentally-induced heart attacks and their treatment. The audience consisted of academicians, practicing cardiologists and specialists in internal medicine, fellows, some CCU nurses, and a sprinkling of medical media people who listened attentively to each ten-minute talk and five-minute question-and-answer period. These meetings were a convenient source of up-to-date information for many physicians, especially those in the academic centers.

For Bergman's talk, he had considerably expanded the 250-word summary that Miller and he had worked on into a four-page paper, which he read slowly, frequently pointing to slides being projected on a huge screen. The talk went off as planned without a hitch, much to his relief, even though he had rehearsed it at the hospital before the staff, and another five times alone in his hotel room. He answered several difficult questions from the audience with dispatch and left the podium feeling elated at his inaugural performance. Returning to his seat, he was still "high" and hardly aware of the other papers that were presented after his, even though one was also from his section. By the time the session concluded, his nervous energy had finally dissipated. He met Miller in the lobby outside the hotel ballroom. Miller was beaming broadly.

"Nice work, Paul. You did a beautiful job, like a true professional. No one would have guessed you're still wet behind the ears. Let me buy you a cup of coffee for a reward?" They moved slowly through the ornate lobby, Miller stopping repeatedly to greet colleagues and well-wishers, shaking hands and backslapping like a politician working the crowd at a Fourth of July picnic. This was the other important function of these meetings—seeing old friends and colleagues. Miller was not only very well-known by many people in the world of medicine, but he was liked and respected.

"Leo!"

"Ben! Good to see you again."

"What's this I hear that you're finally going to get that endowed chair?"

"It's just a rumor, Ben, but one that I'm doing my best to spread." Miller laughed and introduced Bergman to Ben Bernstein, who was in charge of cardiology at Harvard and one of their "competitors" in research endeavors. Bernstein was a much younger man than Miller, but nearly all of his hair was already snowy white. "I'll believe the chair when I get it, Ben. You know I just can't see Harrison Wentworth going down the line for me on this one. Can't see it at all, and it's going to be hard to do it without his support. Not at age 65."

"Unfortunately, Leo, I think you're right on both counts. Say, how's Arlene?"

"She's fine, thanks."

"Why don't the two of you visit us next time you're in Boston?"

"We shall do just that, and I thank you for your invitation."

"Say Leo, before I forget, was Takashi Yamamoto hanging around your shop a few months ago?"

"Yes."

"Mine also. I think you or I might be in line for the big prize his organization hands out."

"I hope it's you, Ben", Miller said with a finality that surprised Bergman. Bernstein moved on and then was lost in the drifting tide of faces and bodies.

"A nice fellow, awfully nice fellow," Miller said. "We've known each other for a long time. He liked your presentation. I was watching him when you were on stage. Don't be surprised if he offers you a junior staff position at Harvard when your fellowship is over."

"You're putting me on, Leo. On the basis of one talk?"

"Yes. That, plus a little snooping into your background and the impression you've made on others during your fellowship, all adds up to a promising young clinician-investigator. That's why, presenting these abstracts is so damn important. But don't let it go to your head; I give you enough compliments as it is. Come on, let's get that coffee."

Bergman spent the rest of the day in a whirl of activities related to the meetings: attending other abstract sessions, a special lecture by Professor Gilbert from London, and visits to the display booths that the drug companies, textbook firms, and medical equipment manufacturers had set up in one of the larger function rooms to show off their wares. Everywhere Bergman went, Miller seemed to pop up sooner or later. This was his sea, and he swam happily from one cove to another, smiling even laughing at times, really enjoying himself as Bergman had seen him do very few times before. The final session of the day was a panel of experts discussing newer treatments of arrhythmias in general, and that was the only time he showed the combative side of his personality.

Sanderson and two of the other fellows joined Bergman in the audience as the panel began to debate the advantages of one protocol over another. One of Ed Smith's senior colleagues from Chicago took the microphone and pointedly attacked the kind of research protocol Miller's group (and others) was using.

"This approach is potentially very harmful," he said. "Reports from Britain have been particularly critical, with several deaths reported."

Bergman watched as Miller bristled. When the speaker suggested the protocol be discontinued, Miller leaped to his feet, grabbed one of the open floor microphones, and soundly rebuffed the speaker. "You have no way of proving the drugs or the procedures killed the patients, who were desperately ill to begin with. How can we proceed with this work if we don't take chances? Those people are like terminal cancer patients with few options for any kind of successful outcome." He went on for several minutes daring the speaker to engage him. When he had finished, Miller stayed at the microphone, chin jutting out, waiting for Smith himself to join in the fray. But if his one-time friend was in the room, he chose not to accept the challenge. The large audience buzzed with excitement at the scene. Finally, seeing there would be no reply—the panelist was fidgeting with his water glass—Miller returned to his seat, no longer agitated, and within a few minutes the session was adjourned.

"What a performance," Sanderson said admirably. "Leo really took it to him."

Bergman agreed. "He's fantastic."

"Better than fantastic. He's a street fighter, when he wants to be, and that's what I like about him and O'Brien too. They're not afraid to mix it up. You know I presented five abstracts at this meeting, don't you? Well, at the last one yesterday, somebody started questioning my results and I went right after him, shouted him down quickly, just like Leo did. I'm like him." Sanderson folded his arms across his chest and nodded his head in agreement. "When I join the faculty..."

"Is that definite?"

"Of course, you bozo. Who else has the papers and presentations that I have?"

"I just..."

"What do you know? One presentation, and you think you're hot stuff? It's not just quality pal, it's quantity. You've got to churn out the stuff."

"Is that the secret? Quantity?" Bergman asked sarcastically. His tone seemed to annoy Sanderson.

He leaned over and whispered in Bergman's ear. "The secret is you do what you have to do."

"For what?"

"For whatever the hell you want, you do what you have to do." With that he got up and left.

CHAPTER

14

Miller thought the meeting had gone very well. He had enjoyed his spat with Smith's associate, he had enjoyed seeing old colleagues, he had been proud of Bergman's presentation—he really liked this young man, he told Arlene—and he continued to be impressed by Sanderson's work. His third-year research fellow gave presentation after presentation with never-ending energy. Miller wanted Bergman to emulate Sanderson as much as possible, but he realized that would be difficult with the restricted research time the first-year fellow had because of his clinical rotations.

Miller was right, and for Bergman the next few months were just as hectic as the proceeding ones. Because of the nature of Bergman's rotation in the cardiac catheterization and non-invasive laboratories, he was now interacting more with Miller's lieutenants than with the leader himself, but in early April he was summoned to Miller's office. Miller was engrossed in conversation with Douglas, but when he saw Bergman waiting outside his open office door, he beckoned him to come in.

One of Miller's strengths in Bergman's eyes was that he rarely beat around the bush. Whatever it was he wanted was soon apparent. Today was no exception. "I'd like Douglas to work with you in O'Brien's lab. We had to double him up on the clinical rotation, and he's missed out on dog work. It might be best if we let him break in with one of your projects. I notice you've arranged to have another two months down there in May and June."

"That's right," Bergman told him. "I switched two months with Adopolous, who wasn't getting along that well with Dr. O'Brien. I didn't think you'd mind."

"Quite the contrary. Better to have someone down there who wants to be there. Can you fit Douglas here into one of the protocols?"

"I don't see why not," Bergman said, after pausing for a moment to consider what he had planned for that time, "and if things are slow for me, I'm sure Sanderson could use him—he seems to be very busy down there now. And he has little use for me."

Miller nodded in agreement. "Sanderson certainly has been a whirlwind in the last six months. But some of the credit belongs to you. I don't know why he's not more appreciative. The way O'Brien tells it to me, it was your device that's enabled things to really take off. That's why I thought Douglas might enjoy working with you. And anyway," he said, trying to keep a straight face, "my spies tell me you're a more pleasant person to work with than either of them." Bergman blushed but said nothing.

Of all the cardiology fellows, Bergman seemed to have the least contact with Douglas and, consequently, felt he didn't really know him. As it turned out, however, he found Douglas to be a very quick learner in the animal laboratory and a more ambitious young man than he had realized. His slow manner of speech was very misleading.

Soon it became apparent that the project Bergman was now working on, essentially a technical refinement of his device, was not exciting enough for Douglas, and he quickly gravitated to where the action was—namely Sanderson. Using Bergman's device and a new drug that Miller's lab had gotten FDA permission to test, Sanderson was turning out study after study using experimental techniques that were surprisingly easy to perform, all with impressive results. Sanderson was ecstatic, even O'Brien was happy, and there was no question that Miller was pleased to see the productivity taking place in the animal research laboratory. Douglas was quickly caught up in the excitement surrounding Sanderson's work and Bergman saw less and less of him as May turned into June. Although Bergman's own interest in the animal laboratory had not abated, it was clear that his plodding work style would not result in a high volume of studies. This didn't bother Bergman. He'd be satisfied if he could just come up with a few high-quality studies to show for his two years of fellowship.

Douglas seemed a bit surprised to see how serenely Bergman took his "partial eclipse" from stardom.

"I never wanted to be a super-star," Bergman explained to him late one afternoon when the two of them were the last to leave the laboratory. "All I wanted to do was make some significant contribution to Miller's research effort. And I think I have."

"But Sanderson's work is the talk of the hospital now. Hey, even the medical students know about it, and that's impressive."

Douglas knew more about Sanderson's work than most of the other fellows, and he seemed genuinely appreciative of the opportunity to work on such an important project, even though he found Sanderson's personality unpleasant at times. "I don't really have any desire to go into research," he said as he neatly folded the reams of graph paper that the afternoon's experiment had generated, "but you never know, man."

"Why are you down here, then?" Bergman asked.

Douglas continued folding. "Miller thought it would be good for me. Even if I didn't like it that much, he said it was a good thing to have on my record when I apply for a job. I take his advice seriously. He was my faculty adviser in medical school and a big help when I was a resident."

"You were lucky to get him for your faculty adviser."

"You're not kidding."

Douglas seemed reluctant to go into it further, but Bergman's curiosity was definitely piqued. After they finished cleaning up, he invited him to the cafeteria for a Coke. "It's on the house," Bergman assured him.

Douglas laughed. "That's all right. I can spring for a can of soda."

"You mean you want to treat me?"

"Hey, any time for a Coke. I'll let you handle the dinners."

They both laughed at the offer and trekked down the basement corridor to the soda machine. The ice-cold tonic made them both gasp with appreciation.

"What made you want to go into cardiology, Bill?"

Douglas thought for a moment. "It's a dynamic field, that's for sure. There aren't too many black cardiologists, that's also for sure. I'm big into community activities as well, so the kind of doctor I'll become is going to be influenced by lots of things, not the least of which will be Miller's advice."

"You really count on him, don't you?

Douglas nodded. "I first got to know Dr. Miller about five years ago," he said. "I was pretty much a radical then, active in a lot of the student organizations that were interested in shaking up the establishment as much as possible. But the one that was nearest and dearest to my heart, and for obvious reasons, was the Black Students Alliance, the BSA. Those were very interesting times." He smiled at the memories the thoughts of the BSA conjured up. "Did you ever hear of us then, the BSA, and the trouble we got into over on the main campus? We made a lot of network news shows."

"No, but that doesn't mean much. I was in New York City five years ago and had a lot of other things on my mind besides campus hijinks on the evening news. What exactly did your group do?"

Douglas smiled again. "What did we do? I guess in reality not very much, at least in retrospect. We didn't blow up buildings or carry guns or things like that from the 60s. Mostly we demonstrated for Black History courses, which we eventually got, Black Pride Week, things like that. It seems pretty tame stuff compared to what went on at other places, but you have to remember that this is a pretty conservative place for a northern school."

"What does that have to do with Leo Miller?"

"Dr. Miller was in the University Senate then, as he is now, representing the Medical School. When we marched on the administration building to protest the school's refusal to let us invite Kwame Nakullah to speak here, we had very little support from the Senate. There were some professors who were with us, but they were more or less discredited in the eyes of the others, because they always supported any radical group, no matter how outlandish. But when Dr. Miller supported us, it changed everything. I mean everything!" Douglas' eyes grew bright. "That's how I got to know him. I admired him so much for what he did that it seemed only natural to take his advice about going to medical school."

"Bill," Bergman said slowly, "I'm having trouble understanding why Leo Miller supported Kwame Nakullah's appearance. I know Nakullah may have been a hero to your group, but you know, as well as I do, that he is perceived as a racist hate-monger by most whites."

Douglas nodded. "I respect your opinion, Paul. I've heard it before, and I guess a lot of people think that way. Even today some blacks do, but five years ago his message was a very powerful one. Dr. Miller didn't support Nakullah's speaking because he agreed with what he was going to say. As far as he was concerned, there was only one issue involved."

"What was that, Bill?"

"Free speech. The First Amendment."

Bergman must have looked startled. "You seem surprised," Douglas said.

"I shouldn't be. It's the business with that woman-bashing sociology professor all over again." He remembered Miller's little lecture on free speech.

"He has very strong ideas on the subject. Maybe you should have a talk with him about it, sometime." Douglas winked slyly.

"I've already been exposed to his views, but I'm learning more about him all the time." Douglas laughed and they called it quits for the day.

CHAPTER

15

Whenever he got the chance during his busy first year of his cardiology fellowship, Bergman found ways to see Jennifer Steiner. Movies, dinners, coffee, snacks—the setting didn't matter as long as they were together. It was only a matter of time before he was saying the words that he knew he would never tell another woman. "I'm falling in love with you," he said one night as they sat in an off-campus restaurant finishing their dessert. She blushed and blew him a kiss across the table. "Me too," she whispered, "more than yesterday and less them tomorrow. It's an old French expression that says exactly how I feel."

"Then it's time isn't it?"

"Are you trying to get into my panties, Dr. Berman?"

"And if I am?"

"Then it certainly is about time!" She laughed again and stood. Ready to go, she put her arm through his. "Your place or mine, monsieur?"

Their first attempt at love-making that night was awkward, but not the second and third times. Lying in bed next to her, Bergman, watching the gentle rise and fall of her full bosom as she slept, realized that his days as a bachelor were over, but he also knew that he had never loved anyone the way he loved Jennifer. Their courtship during that summer of his second fellowship year was a whirlwind one. They were together practically every day of the week, discussing subjects that ranged from politics to the arts, with small doses of psychology and cardiology thrown in for good measure. Over the Labor Day weekend they drove down to Cape Cod and rented a bungalow near Chatham. Unfortunately, neither of them had experienced the vagaries of New England summer weather before. The weekend turned cold and damp, and they spent much of their time in the unheated bungalow huddled around the gas stove for warmth. Undeterred by such minor distractions, their attachment to one another grew stronger as the days passed and, by the beginning of fall, they were ready to let their families announce their engagement. It was planned for a Sunday in early November. Bergman called the local papers with the announcement so that they would have a memento of the occasion.

That Sunday's local newspaper had other news in it that turned out to be of far greater import. On the recommendation of its President, Dr. Takashi Yamamoto, The Japanese Medical Society had decided to award its most prestigious award to Leo Miller, in recognition of his outstanding work in heart-disease research. This award, rarely given to a foreigner, was named the Chrysanthemum Medal, the flower being a symbol of the Imperial Family. In other words, this award, and the huge monetary grant that would go to the university, all came with the blessing of Emperor Hirohito of Japan! Bergman didn't know it at the time, but the announcement of that award and its ties to Hirohito would have almost as much impact on his life as the announcement of his engagement to Jennifer.

CHAPTER

16

January 1945

By the middle of their third year in captivity, the condition of the POWs still alive in the Cabanatuan camp had deteriorated significantly. Thousands had died, and additional thousands had been shipped to Japan as slave laborers. The surprise liberation of the survivors occurred in the still of the night—when the Japanese guards least expected a commando raid— staged by troops who started out from the American lines over 30 miles away. The rescue could not have come at a better time for Miller. After suffering for several weeks with recurrent dysentery that refused to get better, his emaciated frame now carried a body weight of only 95 pounds.

When the shooting began, he was too weak to go to the door of the make-shift infirmary to see what was happening. He lay quietly in his bunk alongside other ill POWs until the door was forced open and six burly American soldiers stormed in. They rapidly surveyed the interior, taking count of who could make the return trip on their own two feet and who would have to be carried out. "I was praying you guys would come," Miller said softly as two of the khaki-clad rescuers covered him with blankets. "Is the whole army here?"

A tall, muscular blond lieutenant scooped up the frail POW and started to carry him out of the building. "Don't tense up. Let yourself relax," the lieutenant said, "and we'll get you out of here okay. No, the whole army is not here, just 120 of us. We're part of the 6th Ranger Battalion, and we've got orders to get you guys back to the American lines. We've got Filipino guerillas waiting outside the camp in case the Japs send reinforcements to stop us."

In the open area in front of the barracks other rescuers were carrying, or helping to carry, all the POWs they could find. "How did you keep going all these years?" the lieutenant asked in amazement, as he and his squad sheltered POWs from the firefights breaking out at the nearby guard towers.

"We never lost hope," Miller whispered. "Doc Larsen wouldn't let us."

"Was Larsen in the barracks with you? Did we get him out?"

"He's dead. He died in October just after we heard about the landings at Leyte. He told us to hang on—there would be landings at Luzon and then we'd be freed. If only he could have hung on a little longer...." Miller choked up and couldn't continue.

"Be thankful we got to you guys in time or you would have joined him. We had good intelligence that the Japs were going to kill all of you when our infantry got closer."

Miller grimaced. "We thought that might happen...Christ, are we glad to see you."

The firefights died down. It was time to go.

"OK, you ready to walk out of here?" the lieutenant asked.

Miller mustered all the strength he could. He would try, he said, but he knew one way or another he would get out of there that night. And, when he did, he also knew that he would never forget what he had gone through. He hoped he would also remember Larsen's admonition not to hate them all, but of that he wasn't so sure.

✝

CHAPTER

17

For the rest of the week, the campus was buzzing with speculation about how the administration was going to use the million-dollar grant that came with the medal. The grant did not come directly from the Japanese Medical Society itself but rather was donated by Japan's largest maker of electronic equipment for medical and scientific purposes. It was an "unrestricted" grant, with which the University could do as it pleased. Immediate speculation was that an endowed chair for Leo Miller would be set up, or, alternatively, the medical-school library would receive a badly needed addition. The latter hope was fueled by a visit to the library from the president of the university and dean of the medical school, a visit that had all the earmarks of an "upgrading" mission.

Even though his summertime rotation in the animal laboratory was long since over, Bergman still tried to spend an occasional late Friday afternoon there to finish up odds and ends from his latest series of experiments. On one Friday in mid-November, not only was he in the lab but so were O'Brien, Sanderson, and Douglas, completing one of Sanderson's latest protocols. Because Sanderson was in the third and final year of his fellowship, he was already being offered junior staff positions at the nation's leading university medical centers based on the quality and quantity of research studies he had done. Miller wanted him to stay and join his own staff. Flushed with the attention being paid to him, Sanderson was in a jovial mood. He had decided to stay in academic medicine, he repeatedly declared to anyone in earshot, despite the lower salaries than those of private practice because it offered more intellectual stimulation. And that was what he wanted—intellectual stimulation.

Where he would eventually go he wouldn't say, but the betting was 2:1 in favor of his remaining with Leo. On this particular Friday, Bergman also joined in the discussion, since his own time of decision was fast approaching. Leo had talked about a third year for him, but he knew if he chose to leave on June 30th, Miller would do what he could to find him a "good" position. It was in the midst of this conversation that Adopolous popped his head into the room.

"Gus, you seem gloomier than usual," Sanderson said laughing. "Not digestive problems, I hope?" There was no love lost between the two of them—Adopolous thought Sanderson pretentious, and in turn Sanderson ridiculed the Midwesterner whenever he could. It was the ugly side of Sanderson, the one that Bergman found extremely offensive.

Gus was upset; that was apparent to all of them.

"Big doing upstairs, guys, and not necessarily the kind of news you like to start a weekend with." All faces turned to him. O'Brien put down his scalpel. "What the fucking hell are you talking about, Adopolous?"

"Miller turned down the Japanese medal."

"What?" O'Brien said in bewilderment. "Why? Did he say why?"

"Personal reasons is all the dean's office would say. No medal and no million-dollar grant."

"What is this personal reasons shit?" Sanderson asked.

"I don't know," Adopolous said, "but I do know the dean's furious and the University president's office is also pissed off at him."

O'Brien flung the scalpel across the room, scaring the daylights out of all of them. "Fuck," he yelled, "Fuck! Fuck! Fuck! I knew in my bones he would do something like this. I knew it; I knew it."

"Why did you think he would turn it down?" Sanderson asked.

"I don't know what's going on inside his head, despite what you guys think. But I do know he was a prisoner-of war in Japan during World War II, and I know he's never forgotten that experience."

"That war was over more than 40 years ago," Douglas said. "What has it got to do with getting an award now?"

O'Brien shrugged. He had nothing more to offer.

The fellows finished what they were doing, cleaned up, and separated for the weekend; each left with his own thoughts ... and questions.

It turned out that Miller's rejection of the award was a source of keen embarrassment to the university. It even led to a minor flare-up of ill feelings between Tokyo and Washington. The award was prestigious; not many had been given out and other Americans had accepted theirs gratefully. Why was Miller such a spoilsport, a lot of people wondered? There was too much about this man Bergman didn't know. He vowed, that the next opportunity he had, he would find out more about the "real" Leo Miller.

Back on the clinical rotation with him, that opportunity came more quickly than he had anticipated. It was shortly before Thanksgiving. He and Jennifer were driving to Boston to spend the holiday with her folks, and then to New York to spend the rest of the weekend with his parents. Bergman arranged for Adopolous to cover the service for him, after, of course, obtaining Miller's approval for such an arrangement. Miller himself would be abroad, so the continuity of care he felt was so important would not be preserved for a few days; hence, the need for his permission.

On the Wednesday before the holiday, Miller invited Bergman to his house to go over some final changes in the manuscript he was preparing about his initial series of experiments with the new heart device. It was to be sent to one of the most prestigious of the medical journals, and Miller wanted to see if he could get it accepted "as is," a rare feat in scientific publishing. After they had been working on the paper for two hours and the antique grandfather clock rang out 11 chimes, Miller decided enough was enough and with a noisy yawn declared the paper finished.

"What about next year?" he inquired as they sat in his study, sipping the vintage port he had grown fond of since his London sabbatical. "Any good offers yet? Harvard interested?"

"No," Bergman answered, "nothing yet."

"Well, then, stay on here. Take a third year, a research year, like Sanderson. If everything goes well, join the staff. This isn't a bad place to put down roots, especially since the newspaper told me you're going to be married soon."

Bergman blushed, embarrassed because he had neglected to inform Miller of his engagement, not thinking he would be interested. Now, Bergman suddenly realized an invitation to their June wedding might be in order, if no more than as a courtesy. First, of course, Miller would have to meet Jennifer.

"Thanks for the offer of a third year," Bergman said, and meant it. Miller had been hinting at it for awhile, but this was the first time he'd made it official—and not just another fellowship year but the prospect of a staff appointment as well. And then, for some reason that he was not sure about—perhaps the effect of the port, the relaxed atmosphere, the sense of accomplishment at finally finishing the manuscript, the pride at being offered a job with Leo Miller—for whatever reason, he felt emboldened enough to ask the question that would unleash the soliloquy that would keep him rooted in his chair for the next hour.

"Dr. Miller..."

"Please, call me Leo. Second-year fellows who share my port are entitled to that, at least..."

"Leo, I know it's none of my business, but what's behind this trouble with the Japanese medal?"

Leo looked at him for a long time before answering. He sipped his port; he took out his pipe, carefully filled the bowl and lit it, puffed long and deep, and then spoke in a low matter-of-fact tone.

"Normally I don't talk about these things, but Arlene tells me every now and then it's good to get things off one's mind. Maybe tonight's as good a time as any. It's certainly been a difficult three weeks for me. One request, Paul: whatever I tell you is between you and me. I like you and I respect you, so don't disappoint me."

Bergman nodded his head and Miller began his soliloquy.

"I was born in 1924 in a small mill town in Massachusetts, not that much different from this one except, of course, there was no university there. I was the older of two brothers. Our parents were shop owners, but very well-read and informed people. My parents' families had left Germany after the failed Revolution of 1848. Very liberal people. During the late 1930s, when I was a teenager, they were very active in anti-Nazi causes, much to the disapproval of many of their fellow citizens of German descent, of which our town had quite a few. They were outspoken opponents of the Fascists in Spain, and they led protest movements against Hitler and picketed German-American Bund meetings. They were called Communists and Jews—neither of which they were—but they didn't care what they were called. Anyway, in those days, you could tell the true Communists because they suddenly stopped being anti-Nazi when Hitler and Stalin signed their non-aggression pact in August, 1939. By contrast, my parents were not at all surprised when the two dictators made their peace.

"When the war started a few weeks later, my parents were firmly on the side of the British and French, and my brother and I were raised in a household in which every war bulletin was carefully followed. Remember, this was during the time that isolationist sentiment was rampant in the United States. Roosevelt—who we worshiped like a God in our household—had his hands full just trying to "lean" towards the British while officially keeping the country neutral. The American First organization was formed—a strange collection of pacifists, like Norman Thomas and right-wing Republican Neanderthals from the mid-west, the heartland of isolation. Charles Lindberg was their spokesmen. My folks despised him, because he had accepted a medal from the Nazis two years earlier. This is how I was brought up, in that atmosphere—the kind of house where patriotism had a very deep meaning, but a good kind of meaning, not a hateful one. My father taught me that the flag was not just the property of the right, it belonged to all Americans; that when Kate Smith sang "God Bless America," it was not written for the Ku Klux Klan and the host of pseudo-Nazi groups who sang it in the '30s—it was for all Americans. Patriotism was not something the left had to be ashamed of, and thank God, I've never forgotten that message."

He stopped to relight his pipe and take a few more puffs before continuing. A faraway look had come to his eyes. Bergman sat there mesmerized, his gaze fixed on Miller's face. "In the spring of 1941, I turned seventeen. The draft was now underway in full force. Roosevelt was preparing the country for a war he knew would come soon, expecting—as we all did—that it would be against Hitler and Germany. I graduated from high school and announced to my parents and 14-year-old brother that I would be enlisting in the army. I needed my parents' consent, and they gave it. This was not a futile stupid adventure like Vietnam—this was Good versus Evil, and when I enlisted I was ready to take on the Nazis as soon as I could. Well, life has a way of playing strange tricks on our pre-arranged plans.

"I joined the army after graduation. I went through basic training and in the fall of 1941 was assigned to, of all places, the Philippines. The Philippines. How the hell was I going to fight Hitler from the Philippines, I wondered? Well, of course, I wasn't. My unit was the 31st Infantry Regiment, a hybrid collection of old-time regular army troops, some new draftees, and a few volunteers like myself. Our morale was good but our weaponry and ammunition stock-piles were not. To make it worse, whatever capabilities the air corps in the Philippines had were completely destroyed when war broke out. MacArthur knew Pearl Harbor had been attacked so we had some warning.

"But our planes were wiped out on the ground anyway. I hope I'm not boring you with this military stuff, but it's necessary to understand the rest of the story. Anyway, when the Japanese army invaded the Philippines, we put up a damn good resistance but somehow our generals got us locked into positions on a long peninsula—Bataan—which didn't exactly give us much freedom of mobility. The Japs wore us down, we ran out of ammunition, food was low. In April of '42, we surrendered. Biggest surrender of an American army since the Civil War. A black day for the Stars and Stripes. The Japanese proceeded to march us off to prison camps.

"I had two close friends in the army, Jack Thomas and Dave Merrigen, both draftees. Jack was from Maine and Dave from New Hampshire—we were sort of a New England trio. They were with me when our unit surrendered, and they were with me when we started on what was to be known as the Bataan Death March. All told there were about 15,000 Americans and 65,000 Filipinos. The Japanese guards were unbelievably brutal. It supposedly goes back to the Japanese belief that "real" soldiers don't surrender, only cowards do, therefore POWS are considered not worthy of respect. As I came to learn, the Japanese also believed—and still do for that matter—that they are the true chosen people; in fact, their ideas about racial purity are not dissimilar at all to those of the Germans. Sort of an Asiatic version of the Aryan race.

"We had to march nearly 70 miles to the POW camps set up for us. Our men died like flies from injuries, disease, starvation—and from Japanese bayonets and Japanese rifle butts. Dave had been ill with dysentery before the march began, and Jack and I helped him as much as we could. We saw what was happening to anyone that fell by the roadside—the Japanese would clobber them to death or bayonet them. We'd been half-carrying Dave for about two days when, at high noon on a blistering-hot day, Jack and I stumbled and the three of us went flying. Jack and I were quickly on our feet, but Dave didn't have the strength to get up. Before we could lift him, a guard's bayonet impaled him through the neck.

"God forgive me, Paul, but I still have nightmares seeing the guards grinning at us. I remember those guards very well. For added measure, they took bayonet swipes at the both of us, missing me but giving Jack a nasty gash across his back. Dave was left to rot by the roadside. Later, we were told that the dead bodies were picked clean by roving hordes of wild dogs. Awful. The rest of the march was a nightmare for Jack because of his slashed back. I kept it as clean as I could and, when we eventually got to our final prison camp, I dedicated myself to keeping him alive after the wound became infected. It was touch and go for weeks, but he made it. A year later he developed malaria and, again, I helped pull him through. In fact, I became sort of unofficial camp doctor, and I suppose that's when I decided I would become one after the war, if I survived.

"When we were finally liberated by Army Rangers in January 1945, there were only 5,000 of the 15,000 still alive. At my camp there were only 500 of us left. I weighed under a hundred pounds. Jack Thomas weighed about 90 pounds. It took us months to regain our strength. By the time I returned home, I was back to 150, so I didn't look too ghastly to my parents. My brother had also enlisted when he turned seventeen in 1944 and had been wounded in Germany, and, as it turned out, both of us finished our recuperation at home. Our family was reunited, safe if not quite sound.

"We had the GI Bill then, so college tuition was free. I wanted to sample life in the big city, so I chose Columbia. My parents didn't really object. After what I had gone through, anything I wanted was fine with them. I loved Columbia—I know you went there too, Paul—so you know the feeling. It was a special time at colleges throughout the country, because the returning GIs brought a sense of maturity to the campuses, a maturity that has not been seen since, I should add. Professors were excited at the prospect of teaching young men who were at college because they really *wanted to learn*, not merely go through a rite of passage to adulthood. And, of course, because of their wartime experience, the returning GIs were *already* adults.

"Yes, it was a great time for me. I had played football in high school, so once I got back to my old playing weight, I played for Columbia. Those were the days when Columbia actually fielded good teams. Lou Little, the coach, was an ornery son-of-a-gun, but he took a liking to me. Even though I was wiry, I was tough. He also knew I had been a Japanese POW. Despite the fact that I was only good enough to be a sub, he saw that I got enough playing time to earn a varsity letter in 1946, which was damned nice of him, because I messed up my knee in the famous 1947 Army game and never played again. After that, it was medical school and cardiology training and the rest you know.

"I have to apologize for being so long-winded. I know you didn't ask me about all that, you asked me about the medal. It just takes me a while to get there." He glanced at his watch. "It's almost one a.m., so I'll sum it up. All through the death march, all through the prison camps, we heard nothing from our captors except the supremacy of the Japanese people and their Emperor. After the war I became a student of that whole period. I became convinced that the Emperor was no passive participant in the preparations for war or the conduct of the war. As far as I'm concerned—and I'm far from alone in this—Emperor Hirohito was a war criminal, just like Prime Minister Tojo was and we hanged him in 1946. Feeling that way, I agonized for a week when I learned about this medal. Then I spoke to my old buddy, Jack Thomas, who's still alive and owns an insurance agency right across the state line in his hometown, in Connecticut. Jack thought I should discuss it with our mutual friends in the American Legion." He suddenly stopped when he saw Bergman's expression change. "You look surprised, Paul." Bergman spoke for the first time since Miller began to talk.

"You, in the American Legion? You, the guy that defended Bill Douglas and the BSA? I'm incredulous."

"You shouldn't be. Being narrow-minded is not one of my faults. The flag belongs to all of us. Anyway, when I met with the American Legion chapter, Jack reminded me that I'm also a charter member of the Defenders of Bataan and Corregidor, a group of old-timers who occasionally meet to reminisce. Jack also reminded me that I had a duty to Dave Merrigan and all the others, who died on the march and in the POW camps and that no matter how many buildings and businesses the Japanese took over in America and no matter how much money they donated to American universities, there was one thing they could never buy—the forgiveness of those that Japan had brutalized. After I heard Jack's eloquent plea, I really had no choice. Did I, Paul? Did I really have a choice?"

He didn't really expect Bergman to answer, the question was for himself, and he had already answered it. His pipe had gone out for the last time that night. No need to relight it.

"I have no regrets, whatever the university administration may think of me."

"But you're friends with Dr. Yamamoto and he's Japanese."

"I learned not to hate all Japanese. Major William Larsen, my inspiration during the POW years—and a big reason why I became a doctor—taught me that before he died in 1944. I have nothing against individual Japanese. Takashi's a fine man. I wish he hadn't nominated me for this award. That's what I was concerned about when he visited us in his "official capacity," as he put it. Maybe I should have said something then about not accepting it, but it seemed presumptuous. I hope I haven't embarrassed him too much. I really antagonized over this. Maybe if Hirohito were dead I could do it. But as long as this medal is in the name of Emperor Hirohito I can't accept it. Hirohito's a war criminal in my mind."

"Anything I can do to help?"

Miller reflected for a moment.

"Nothing now, thanks anyway. Who knows, I may take you up on that one day. Who knows, life is funny that way. Good night, Paul."

"Life is funny that way." There was a déjà vu aspect to that phrase. Where had Bergman heard it before? He wondered as he drove home. Later that night it would come to him—memories of a long-ago Thanksgiving night with his family in front of a TV set and his father saying those words.

CHAPTER

18

As if by special dispensation, the arrival of the cold weather in December distracted the campus from its fascination with the drama swirling around the rejected award. The Administration issued no further statements, no further rumors circulated in the hospital about punishment for Miller. For his part, Leo Miller seemed content to let the issue slide into the past.

Instead, he immersed himself in preparations for the next month's annual meeting of the National Cardiology Society. This year, the NCS would meet in Atlanta. Sanderson was Miller's star performer. He had his name on seven abstracts, a noteworthy accomplishment for someone who was still a fellow. Four papers on the program were to be presented by him, another two by a student working in his lab, and a seventh one by O'Brien himself. Two more clinical papers relating to patient care (new drug trials) were also on the program from Miller's group. All in all, there were nine papers with Miller's name on them. In addition, he was moderating an abstract presentation session, chairing a symposium, and giving one of the keynote addresses in the huge arena area of the Georgia Convention Center. Miller had never participated in a cardiac meeting before in which he was so much in the spotlight.

During the course of December, the abstract rehearsals were scheduled every week, except for the week between Christmas and New Year's. Miller wanted the 10-minute presentation perfect—in style, content, and in timing. He personally inspected each slide mock-up before it was finalized. He goaded the speakers unmercifully with questions when they had finished their trial presentations. When they left for Atlanta, he wanted them prepared to answer any question the audience could come up with. He knew there would be both "friends" and "enemies" hanging on his presenters' every word. Miller's time was precious—he couldn't be everywhere at once—so he asked Bergman to sit in for him on the rehearsals and be as critical as possible. Bergman was especially severe in some of the questioning directed at Sanderson. It was not done in malice, though Sanderson began to think so.

"Why do you have it in for me, Paul? Not jealous by any chance?"

"Don't be silly. I'm supposed to prepare you for hostile fire in Atlanta. You're supposed to thank me for making sure you're prepared for anything."

"It seems to me that you're enjoying your work a little too much," Sanderson fumed. "Remember yesterday, when you asked me about those two outlying points on the graph? You almost seemed to relish watching me squirm to explain them. I was really embarrassed when I had to ask Bill Douglas if he remembered the particulars of those experiments, because I surely didn't."

"But that's the point! Those are exactly the kinds of questions someone's bound to ask. Anyway, I wouldn't worry about it. In all your papers I've heard, those are the only two points that didn't fit on or near the regression line. Anyone with results that good doesn't have to worry about two measly outliers. No one can be perfect, you know."

Sanderson shrugged. "I guess you're right. I wouldn't want to be perfect." For some reason, the thought seemed to cheer him up, and when he left, he was smiling.

The Atlanta meetings began a week after New Year's Day, and they were a rousing success for Miller's clinical and research units. Bergman didn't attend (it was his turn to "mind the store"), but he heard all about it from Adopolous.

"I've never seen Miller happier," Gus told Bergman over pizza one frigid night with Jennifer and Gus's wife, Daphne. "He was the center of attention wherever he went. His opening address received as much applause as I've ever heard."

"Well, you haven't been to that many meetings," Daphne said sharply. She and Gus never seemed to call a truce in their perpetual sniping attacks.

"True," Gus admitted, "but it was still awesome. And best of all, no one in Ed Smith's Chicago crowd said a word."

Remembering back to the previous year's meeting in New York, Bergman knew how pleased Miller must have been with that development.

"I'm glad Dr. Miller had a successful meeting," Jennifer said, toying with her pizza crust, "because if he's in a good mood, the odds are good you'll all be better off."

"Nothing like a psychologist to put everything in its proper light," Adopolous said laughing. "Here's a toast to the future Mrs. Dr. Bergman."

Jennifer corrected him. "Forget that Mrs. Dr. stuff. Just call me Dr. Bergman, or maybe Dr. Steiner-Bergman, I haven't decided."

Gus groaned. "Oh, my God, a hyphenated wife. That's all Paul needs."

They all shared in the laughter, but Bergman wasn't quite sure if Jennifer was joking. She had been talking about the hyphen on and off for two weeks.

At that moment the noise in the pizza parlor suddenly ceased. From the kitchen, Frankie, the owner, appeared with a huge birthday cake in his hands. His assistant turned down the lights and the customers—a mixed band of students, junior faculty, and assorted medical personnel—broke into "Happy Birthday."

"This is for you, Doc," Frankie said to Bergman. "A present from your girlfriend."

Jennifer blushed. "Hey Frankie, I'm supposed to tell him that, not you."

"Sorry, miss." Frankie obviously still had to be educated about feminism, but since he was a product of the "old country," Jennifer excused him that night. Actually, Bergman thought it was a nice treat on her part, and the four of them, along with anyone else who wanted a piece of cake, enjoyed themselves immensely.

When Bergman walked Jennifer home later, he felt more strongly than ever that he was a very lucky man.

"I don't want to wait for June," he told her at her door. "Let's get married at the end of March. If our folks don't agree, we'll elope."

He expected her to object, but she didn't. "The sooner the better," she agreed. They knew they were decidedly old-fashioned; it seemed everyone else was living together for years before tying the knot. But they weren't kids; they knew when they had found what they wanted. Living together wasn't necessary. One long kiss and then Bergman went back to his room, because it was his turn to be on call from midnight on. Not much of a birthday treat, he thought, as he lay in bed staring out at the moonlit sky, but he wasn't much for birthdays anymore. He did know he was happy, happier than he had ever been in his 32 years.

CHAPTER

19

Bill Douglas cornered Bergman immediately after morning rounds the very next day. "I've got to talk to you," he said urgently, "someplace private."

There really wasn't any place that was private; fellows didn't have their own offices, just cubicles with desks and lockers in common changing areas. It was too cold to walk outside the hospital. Finally, Douglas suggested a place, the main auditorium. No lectures were in progress and it was deserted. They flicked on the lights and sat in the front row immediately in front of the podium where famous homegrown and visiting professors had regaled audiences with their scientific exploits.

"All right, Bill, you have my undivided attention for the next 15 minutes and 30 seconds," Bergman said jovially. "What's on your mind?"

Douglas's features reflected concern. "It's hard to know where to start, but I just have this funny feeling there's something fishy going on in the animal lab."

"Something fishy is kind of vague."

"I know, but I feel I can trust you even with concerns that aren't well-defined. That's why I've decided to confide in you and no one else. At least, for the time being. "

"I'm listening."

"Last month during the rehearsals for the NCS meeting in Atlanta, I appreciated for the first time the extent of Sanderson's work in the dog lab. It is really impressive."

Bergman nodded. Douglas was right; it was impressive.

"As I sat there listening to one presentation after another about the animal experiments he was supervising or assisting or advising on, a little alarm bell went off in my head. There were just too many. That's what I meant by a something-fishy feeling. After the rehearsals were over, I made a note to myself to follow-up on this hunch. This month, when the abstract booklet came out in Atlanta, I added up the number of dogs used in the seven experimental protocols that Sanderson was involved in. The figure was 135."

"So?"

Douglas leaned forward, dropping his voice even lower. "Remember, Sanderson's protocols were not the only ones being tested. You had some, and O'Brien had his own. Yet despite that, I'm sure the total number of dogs ordered was nowhere near 135."

"What are you suggesting?"

"One of two things could have happened. Either Sanderson piggybacked one protocol on another protocol—you know, using the data for more than one study; or something worse, like using one set of control dogs for half a dozen papers."

"Not exactly cricket," Bergman said, "but if you state it in your methods section of a paper, that's usually adequate."

"True," Douglas said, "but I have a feeling that was only part of it. Actually, I think Sanderson was purposely inflating the number of dogs he said he was experimenting on. I can't prove it, and I hate myself for thinking it, but I do."

"Ridiculous," Bergman told Douglas. "But, if you have doubts, why don't you sit down with O'Brien and discuss it with him?"

"Actually, I sort of alluded to it yesterday. He got very upset with me. That's why I came to you. I can't go to Dr. Miller with something as flimsy as this, but I can go to you. You have a good rapport with O'Brien. He'll at least listen to you."

Bergman said nothing but thought of the implication of what he had just learned. Either Douglas had stumbled onto something that would be very embarrassing—at the very least—for the reputation of the medical school and all concerned, or the whole affair was a simple misunderstanding. The easiest thing to do was to wash his hands of it and insist that Douglas sit down with O'Brien or Miller. But with any allegation of misconduct in his lab, he knew O'Brien would fly off the handle and become completely irrational, as he had done on other occasions. Miller, on the other hand, would be dispassionate throughout, but would not take kindly to Douglas if his accusation turned out to be false. "Character assassination," he would call it, and Douglas' stock would fall drastically.

No, the easy way out was not really an option. Bergman would have to make some time and look into it himself.

"I'll help you," he told Douglas, "but only on one condition."

"What's that?"

"If I find there's nothing to it, you'll drop the matter."

Douglas thought for a minute before responding. Finally, he said "agreed," and they shook hands on it.

"Where would you like to start?" Douglas asked.

"I want to go over the logs where all the animals are registered when they arrive in the lab."

Douglas agreed. Bergman looked at his watch. It was almost time for the afternoon ECG conference. The first chance he would have to go to the animal lab would be at five o'clock. He arranged with Douglas to meet him there then.

Eddy, the technician who ran O'Brien's animal laboratory, was a 40-year-old ex-alcoholic. Eddy had been a boxer once, and the combination of his pugilistic scars and the ravages of alcohol made him look like 60. Despite the rugged exterior, Eddy's blue eyes twinkled and a smile never seemed far away. He knew he was lucky to be alive and lucky to have a decent job. The person he owed the most to was O'Brien and although his personality was diametrically opposed to that of his mercurial lab director, they got along famously. Bergman knew Eddy would never countenance any suspicions of malfeasance directed at his boss, so the first thing he did when he and Douglas entered the lab was to reassure Eddy on that score.

"We need to check some logs, but what we are doing has nothing to do with Dr. O'Brien," he said as soothingly as possible. "It's only concerned with Dr. Sanderson. We have to go through the records of his experiments."

"Then why won't you let me tell Dr. O'Brien what you're doing?" The look on Eddy's battered face was neither hostile nor supportive, merely inquisitive.

"Because he'll go crazy at the very thought of someone cheating on him and Dr. Miller. Won't he, Eddy? You know it and I know it. The best thing to do is to first see if there's anything to it. There's time enough to get him involved if we find something that's out of line."

Eddy pondered what Bergman said, again without showing any emotion. His answer came in the form of a brief nod of his head. Whatever his reason, he had decided to help them. Out came the ledgers from the wall cabinets, one after another, until there were four thick books sitting on an empty desk top.

"I'm going to get a cup of coffee," Eddy said with a wink. "Keep an eye on the lab for awhile."

"Sure, Eddy."

The three of them understood that when Eddy returned, he expected the audit to be finished. He would then put the ledgers back in their cabinets and lock up the lab for the night. If O'Brien walked in while the fellows were doing their checking, they would have to do the explaining, not Eddy.

"You take two and I'll take two," Bergman told Douglas. "Find all the entries from the time Sanderson started in the lab two and a half years ago. Keep a count on this sheet of paper."

Two or three dogs were delivered from the city pounds once or twice a month for research purposes. Their care and feeding were expensive, so detailed records were kept as to their condition and disposition. It was relatively easy to determine that in the time period they were considering, a total of 92 dogs had been purchased by the laboratory. Douglas was right. There was something wrong. Sanderson reported the results of 135 experiments, yet O'Brien's own experiments, plus Bergman's had accounted for at least 30 additional dogs. Considering the number that died in failed experiments, there should have been about 200 dogs purchased.

"We're reporting on almost twice as many dogs as we've actually purchased." Bergman rubbed his temples and grimaced.

Douglas leaned back. "Then I was right."

"You're right," Bergman conceded, shaking his head in disgust. What should he do next, he wondered?

That night, the more Bergman reflected on the afternoon's events, the more he tossed and turned. He wanted to find some logical explanation for the discrepancy in the animal count, but try as he might, no explanation presented itself. He was either going to have to speak to Sanderson himself—which he did not want to do, at least not yet—or to O'Brien—which he wanted to do even less—or he was going to have to do some further investigating on his own.

Dropping the issue, and thereby leaving Douglas out on a limb, was no longer a viable option. Nor, for that matter, was approaching Miller without having a firmer grasp of the facts. The only person who really "knew" everything that went on in the animal laboratory was Eddy. Sooner or later Bergman would have to sit down with him. With that much at least decided, he finally fell asleep.

When he awoke in the morning, a thin layer of snow covered the ground, and more heavy wet flakes were falling without let-up. Southern New England was having its first snowstorm of the year. That night was the dean's annual reception, and for the first time in several years, boots were appropriate footgear. Jennifer didn't mind. Romping in the drifts was her idea of fun. Bergman's own tastes were a bit more sedate.

"You're an old fuddy-dud at 32," she chided him.

"Love me or leave me," he answered, while ducking one of her poorly aimed snowballs.

"I think I'll try and get you drunk tonight. Maybe that will loosen you up a bit." She stuck her tongue out and threw one last frozen missile his way, almost hitting him.

Getting Bergman drunk that night was not difficult. The dean's office supplied all manner of beer, wine, and liquor, which, combined with skimpy hors d'oeuvres, soon had most of the guests more than a little tipsy. Miller and his wife were right in the midst of the throng, glad-handing all those they came in contact with, reminding Bergman of Miller's participation in the NSC meetings: he wondered if he and Jennifer would ever be able to do it as effectively—assuming, of course, he chose to go into academic medicine. He had wanted Jennifer to meet Miller and Arlene and this seemed as good a time as any. They inched their way closer as the circle of partygoers around Miller gradually contracted. Miller was in such a good mood that it seemed no one could cast a pall over this private party, but one person did and that was none other than the host himself, the dean.

Jennifer and Bergman and several of the cardiology fellows were now standing close enough to hear most of Miller's conversation with his boss.

Jack Smiley was the dean. Still possessing an abundant supply of red hair, Smiley was an imposing figure as he strode about the party room, shaking hands and conversing with his guests. His voice was deep and resonant, his language often blunt and sometimes coarse. He was an old friend of Harrison Wentworth. In fact, rumor had it that it was only because of Smiley that Wentworth had been appointed Chief of Medicine. Their friendship had been formed at the Ivy Club at Princeton. Over the years, those ties grew stronger as they progressed up the academic ladder. When Smiley left Yale to take the deanship, he made no secret of his dissatisfaction with the then Chief of Medicine. Harrison Wentworth's appointment followed within a year. Where Wentworth was perceived as weak, Smiley was feared.

"Well, Leo, are you enjoying our winter wonderland out there?"

"I was never a great lover of snow, Jack."

"And what about you, Arlene, are you a winterite?"

"Hardly," Arlene said, nursing her eggnog.

"Wonderful, "Smiley said with a touch of sarcasm. "A beautiful winter day and evening brings no appreciation at all from the Millers. I suppose you'd rather be on a warm beach in some Caribbean island?"

"Not a bad idea, Jack."

"That's funny, Leo, I would have thought you'd have gotten your fill of warm beaches after your stint in the Philippines. From everything I've heard, the experience was so unpleasant it still rankles you years later."

"What's that supposed to mean, Jack? Are you going to start in on me for that Japanese medal again?"

Smiley jutted his chin out and advanced on Miller. "I haven't forgotten about it. Your goddamn Jap-bashing cost me a new library addition and embarrassed the hell out of the whole university administration. The president still curses you every time some bureaucrat in Washington calls up with a new complaint about your tactless behavior."

"That's not fair!" Arlene said angrily. "What Leo did, he did for good reasons." Smiley remained belligerent. "Your husband's living in the past. The war's over, Arlene. We're all allies now. We use Japanese TVs and Japanese automobiles. Or are you too uppity to buy Japanese goods?"

"We try not to," Miller said evenly. "If an American company makes an equally good product, we'll buy the American product or a German one—or Korean or Chinese."

"I drive a Honda," the dean said loudly. "What do you drive?"

"I drive a Buick, I like the roomy interior," Miller replied softly. "Look, Jack, I thought the matter was settled months ago. I had to do what I thought best. Surely, you can understand that?"

Smiley groaned. "Christ, I remember that lecture from the Black Student Alliance fiasco. So don't give me that crap about your principles, Leo. You think the rest of us don't have principles? You bet we do. But we're not holier-than-thou breast-beaters who have nothing better to do than harbor fantasies about revenging antique wrongs."

"What's done is done," Miller said in a low voice, aware of the listeners around them. "I'm sorry if the award business caused trouble."

Scowling, Smiley shook his head from side to side. "Yeah, it caused trouble. That's for sure." Wentworth now approached the two of them and put his hand on Smiley's shoulder. "Great party, Jack, as usual."

"Thanks, Harrison. Leo and I were just talking about the importance of principles. Leo's a firm believer in them."

"Aren't we all, Jack?"

"My point exactly."

The dean and the chief of medicine waited for Miller to say something; he just stared into his drink. Arlene finished her eggnog and brushed at a nonexistent stain on her jacket. The noise of the party continued unabated around the four of them.

Finally, the dean shuffled off to another group, Wentworth in tow.

"We don't need this aggravation," Arlene whispered.

"No," Miller agreed. "I also have a distinct feeling that my endowed chair may not be such a sure thing."

"Don't be silly. They wouldn't use something like this ..."

"They're just looking for an excuse," Miller said matter-of-factly, "and I think I may have provided them with one. They'll probably use the money for my chair to refurbish the library since they don't have the Japanese money; they can then rationalize that it serves me right."

Contrary to what he had been led to believe by Adopolous, and after witnessing the hostility of Smiley, Bergman couldn't believe the ill-feelings were all about Arlene, or O'Brien's vomiting on Harrison Wentworth's rugs. No, they disliked Miller for other reasons, reasons that perhaps predated the Japanese medal fiasco but were most certainly exacerbated by it. And the reasons were not going to go away. This was certainly not the time to burden Miller with Douglas' suspicions.

"Excuse me, Dr. Miller," he said loudly, as if to announce their presence. "I'd like to introduce you to my fiancé, Dr. Jennifer Steiner."

Miller's face lit up at the sight of Jennifer's ear-to-ear smile. Even Arlene grew more cheerful.

"You've got a great catch there, young lady," Miller said earnestly.

"And I'm sure that goes for Dr. Bergman as well, dear." Arlene would not let the distaff side down.

"Thank you, Mrs. Miller," Jennifer said elbowing Berman playfully.

"You said Doctor," Arlene went on. "Does that mean medical doctor?"

"Psychologist," Jennifer replied. "Ph.D. takes longer to get than an M.D."

"Even better," Miller chimed in. "We have enough medical doctors already. Need more head doctors, if you ask me. Especially at this party."

It was Arlene's turn to deliver an elbow.

"Good luck to both of you," she said, and the two then drifted off toward the food table. Bergman hardly had time to collect his thoughts when Sanderson and his date suddenly appeared in the Millers' wake.

"This must be the next Mrs. Bergman," Sanderson said in greeting.

"The first and only, I hope." Jennifer said tartly.

Sanderson introduced them to his date Vicki, the pert and leggy redhead who Bergman remembered from the nurses' party. "This is a great party," Sanderson announced cheerfully. "Every mover and shaker in the medical school is here."

"Very exalted company," Bergman agreed. "We lowly fellows should be honored to even be included."

"Speak for yourself," Sanderson said quickly. "Some of us aren't so lowly. Seven abstracts—not exactly chopped liver." He snapped imagined suspenders.

The women laughed and Sanderson grinned in delight. "What's the matter, Bergman, you getting those pangs of jealousy again?"

His date kicked Sanderson in the leg, "Stop being obnoxious," Vicki said.

Bergman bowed to her. "My dear, I couldn't agree with you more."

"What the hell do I care what you think, anyway?" Sanderson said to Bergman, a huge grin still on his face. "One of these days I'll be a mover and shaker too."

Jennifer's ears perked up. "Is being famous that important to you?"

Sanderson reflected a moment. "Is it better to be rich than poor? It's the same thing with prestige. Most of us would rather have it than not have it. Is it an all-consuming desire of mine? Of course not, but I wouldn't mind a little more of it now that I've finally experienced the first few accolades of recognition. Is that so horrible?" he asked again.

"Of course not," Bergman answered, but Sanderson's bravado irritated the sores Eddy's log books had opened.

Bergman and Jennifer headed for the punchbowl exchanging giggles. "Wow. Is he really that narcissistic?" Jennifer asked.

"What you see is what you get."

"I'm off to the ladies room. Have a drink on me."

No sooner was she gone then Bergman was approached by Wentworth, a broad smile on his face. "Good to see you again Dr. Bergman. You and Dr. Sanderson are bringing welcome attention to our institution. More than I can say for your boss."

"Well, I . . ."

"It's okay. I saw you standing nearby while Leo and the dean had words. It's only natural to be defensive, but I think you see what we're up against with his arrogance. I have good contacts with other Chairs around the East, so when you're ready to head out on your own, let me know. Just remember, staying too long with Leo may not be your best option." With an enigmatic wink he was gone.

CHAPTER

20

Sanderson left the party in a huff. He had not taken kindly to the mild put-down that Bergman's fiancé had administered. Who did that psychologist—not even MD for crying out loud—think she was dealing with?

"She embarrassed me in front of the medical school big-wigs," he told his date, but Vicki would have none of it.

"You behaved like an asshole," she declared, "you deserved what you got."

Sanderson stopped suddenly, his frigid breath hanging in front of him in a fine mist as he surveyed his companion. "Now, *you're* in my face? If I have to fight everyone else, I don't need you to pick this time to desert me." They walked silently in the light snow.

When he finally spoke, the words came out in a rush, so fast that she had trouble hearing them clearly. But later, when the police questioned her, she was amazed that she was able to remember his sentences almost word for word. "I love to beat that guy," Sanderson said. "I love to beat him with words and articles and whatever it takes. Miller's taken a liking to him—he might even give that faculty position to him, not me. I have to do whatever it takes to beat him out even if I . . . ." His words trailed off.

"What does that gibberish mean?" the red-head recalled asking, not sure what the rambling was all about. Writing more papers? Or something more ominous? But from that point until he bid her goodnight, Sanderson said no more, and no matter how much she persisted over the next few weeks he would not answer her question.

CHAPTER

21

On a Thursday morning in early February, Leo Miller called all the staff and fellows into the conference room.

"The animal research carried out by Drs. Sanderson and O'Brien and others has been especially gratifying in that the results seem to support my hypothesis that the new anti-arrhythmic agents will be effective in humans. Dr. Sanderson has several manuscripts at press and is preparing several others. But even before they are officially published in the journals, I've felt the results were important enough to communicate them to the National Institutes of Health. The NIH chief, who fortunately is a cardiologist by training, attended the NCS meeting in Atlanta and heard Sanderson's presentation. On the basis of what he heard, and the preprints of the manuscripts we provided him, he wants to fund a large multicenter international clinical study with the core laboratory at our hospital. Naturally, we are delighted with these developments."

He paused and looked around the room at the full array of his clinical and research staff, fellows and faculty. "I cannot tell you how important this undertaking will be. I'm going to be calling on several of you for help in organizing the NIH pilot study. A lot of work is involved, but the possible benefit in patient care is enormous."

Bergman was reminded of Mrs. Wilson, the unfortunate woman who had died during his first summer on Miller's service. As he recalled, it had also affected Miller, even though she was just one of hundreds of such patients he had taken care of in his many years of cardiology practice. To think that a breakthrough was now possible (thanks indirectly to his providing the animal lab with the device that was used to cause the experimental heart attacks) was both humbling and, at the same time, immensely satisfying. It almost made up for Sanderson not including his name on any of the abstracts.

The meeting broke up and the fellows went back to their assignments. Even though Bergman was not involved in the animal laboratory that month, he realized he was going to have to go back there as soon as possible to find out what had happened to the "missing" dogs. The whole NIH multicenter grant was based on this animal data.

The publication that week of the first of Sanderson's experiments was helpful because, in the methods section, he had several charts showing how each of the dozen dogs he was reporting on had fared through the various maneuvers. It seemed the simplest thing to do was to go over the records detailing those experiments. The actual lab sheets with the raw data (pressure tracings and the like) were always kept by the investigator for at least several years after the studies were published. Some researchers were even known to keep their records forever. Bergman assumed that Sanderson had his records somewhere in the lab. How to approach him about checking them was another matter. To do so directly could mean an ugly confrontation—not that Bergman suspected he didn't have such records, but because all his pent-up anger at Bergman's nit-picking in the past would now be unleashed at the idea that Bergman suspected he was doing something wrong.

The more he thought about it, the more sense it made to approach O'Brien first. After all, he was Sanderson's supervisor and ultimately would want to know if there was problem in the lab—his lab.

Bergman found O'Brien sitting in his office at the back of the laboratory, poring over a brochure describing the upcoming sports car races at Glenn Falls, New York. His feet were up on his desk; a pencil dangled from his mouth.

"I have a feeling I can actually win one of these things in the spring," he said when he saw Bergman. "I've never done that you know. Closest I've come is second."

"How long have you been racing?"

O'Brien thought for a moment. "Twelve years, first, down in Tennessee, then up here."

"Are you ever scared?"

"All the time, but I do it anyway. Some day it will probably kill me, but what the hell, it's better than dying in bed."

O'Brien always seemed uncomfortable making small talk, so Bergman wasn't surprised when his tone changed and he said almost curtly, "Well, what can I do for you?"

Bergman sat down in the chair beside his desk. "I have reason to believe that Dr. Sanderson is not reporting his data properly." He felt awkward saying those words, but he continued anyway. "Since you're the director of the animal lab, I thought you ought to know about it."

"What kind of shit is this?" O'Brien said angrily. For a moment, Bergman wasn't sure whether the "shit" meant the prospect of finding falsified data or presenting him with such a story.

"Who the hell are you to be casting suspicions on Sanderson's work? What gives you the right?"

Not wanting to drag Eddy into this quagmire—at least, not yet—Bergman chose his words carefully. "All I'm suggesting is that you might want to check the raw data on the series of experiments just published in the *Annals of Cardiology*. If everything is O.K., then I'll make sure the matter is resolved without any further interference."

"I can't believe you're sitting there saying these things."

"Look, Dr. O'Brien," Bergman said, hoping to sound as exasperated as he felt. "I'm doing this to avoid a problem, not cause one. I'm trying to allay suspicions. But I can't see how I can surreptitiously look at the raw data without getting Sanderson all fired up. And if I don't allay these suspicions, the person who confided in me will end up in Dr. Miller's office. That will have the same end result as my visit with you, but it will also get Dr. Miller involved—and probably upset him as well—whether or not any impropriety occurred."

Bergman thought that prospect would sober O'Brien up, but it didn't.

"Leo doesn't get himself involved in dog lab experiments," O'Brien said tartly. "That's my domain, and he leaves me alone. So if your source has a problem with our studies, Leo will probably send him or her to me directly, which would not be the worst idea I've heard this week. I'd like to get my hands on this troublemaker. You're right, I shouldn't waste my time and energy on you, the messenger. Get the fuck out and tell your whistle-blower that no one in my lab has ever done anything improper, nor will they ever. I run a good lab." His feet were off the desk now, and his face was contorted with anger. "Do I make myself clear?"

Shaking, Bergman retreated. No one had entered the lab during O'Brien's outburst, so there were no witnesses to Bergman's dressing-down. The rest of the day he moved as if drugged. Jennifer noticed the difference at dinner that night in her apartment. She didn't beat around the bush.

"What happened today, Paul? You look like you've seen a ghost."

Bergman told her about the false dog numbers and then recounted the day's events.

"What do I do now?" he said aloud, only half expecting an answer from her. It was more for his own sake. "Go to Miller? Or let sleeping dogs lie? Forgive the pun."

"Whatever you do, or don't do, sooner or later Bill Douglas will come around for an accounting. You'll have to justify to him whatever decision you come to."

She was right, but at the time the easiest thing was to do nothing. Bergman didn't have the courage to face O'Brien again, and he couldn't see going to Miller. O'Brien must have said something to Sanderson, because in the next few days there was a flurry of activity in the animal lab. But it was not the kind of activity Eddy and Douglas were used to. Sanderson began his experiment as usual, ran off reams of recording paper, then abruptly terminated the experiment and began another. This behavior by itself was bizarre enough, but both Eddy and Douglas observed him marking the pressure tracing with a date from the previous year! He made no attempt to hide what he was doing.

Neither Eddy nor Douglas understood what the purpose of the post-dating was, but when Douglas told Bergman what was occurring, he knew immediately that his hunch had been correct: the raw data on the series of experiments reported in the *Annals of Cardiology* was either non-existent or incomplete. Sanderson was filling the void.

Sure enough, when the February issue of the *American Cardiac Journal* appeared with another of his studies, the same retro chart-dating activity reoccurred.

O'Brien was either ignorant of it, or didn't want to know it was going on, because he made no comment about it at the weekly research conference. Sanderson didn't seem at all perturbed, and since he directed no especially venomous glares Bergman's way, Bergman assumed O'Brien hadn't told him that he was the source of the rumors. Obviously though, he had told Sanderson something.

He again confided his concerns to Jennifer that night. "Something's come over Sanderson. He's like a man possessed. I don't know exactly what O'Brien told him, but he's got sort of a wild look in his eyes at times and at other times he's whistling to himself like he's king shit. Meanwhile his hair is growing long, and he's not shaving regularly. If you thought he was creepy when you first met him, you should see him now."

"He's really bugging you isn't he?" Her voice was concerned.

"Of course!"

"Then let's get the hell out of here and go to the Caribbean for a week. Get Gus or one of those other guys to cover you on the clinical service, and let's sit in the sun and drink tequilas and then jump into bed and screw like bunnies!"

"Jennifer!"

"Stop being a fuddy-dud! Let's do it. I guarantee that will cheer you up."

"I've got an even better idea. Let's get the university chaplain's office to find us a rabbi, and we'll turn the winter vacation into an elopement."

"But our parents..."

"... will understand."

And, after some minor grumbling, both sets of parents gave their blessings.

The Doctors Bergman chose the Virgin Islands for their get-away retreat. The water was a clean and sparkling turquoise, ideal for their daily ritual: they would sunbathe, swim, read, swim again, and then—after exchanging knowing glances—walk hand-in-hand to their rented beachside cottage. Quickly disrobing, he licked the salt off each part of her body, while she moved in anticipatory delight as he caressed her lips, her nipples, and finally her pubic area. She came very quickly—

and repeatedly—as soon as he entered her. Then, back out to the beach to nap in the shade, wake up, and do it all over again, but now it was her tongue doing the work, starting with his lips and stopping only long enough at his loins to allow him to release himself with a sudden orgasmic jolt.

Thus went the days and nights of pure ecstasy.

CHAPTER

22

When he returned from his honeymoon, Bergman was rested, happy, and very much enjoying married life. Jennifer set up housekeeping in a large apartment they had hastily rented, while he made arrangements to sublet their old apartments.

Tanned and (temporarily) satiated of sexual desires, Bergman returned to work to be met by envious stares from his colleagues, most of whom were deep in the throes of the winter blahs, complete with doughy pallor. In New York, the month of March was already an invitation to spring; in New England, it was a different story. Winter storms still howled with annoying regularity as they progressed east from the Great Lakes or south from Canada. Despite the miserable conditions on the campus and in the town, life at the hospital and medical school continued at a frenetic pace. The cardiology staff was particularly obsessed with the preparation of the proposal for the multicenter clinical research study. Even though the NIH had given them the green light to embark on the plan, the actual document still had to be meticulously prepared.

Bergman was assigned a large chunk of the methodology section. Specific guidelines had to be followed, and the separate section written with both detail and clarity. This time-consuming task distracted him from his determination to tell Miller all that he suspected about Sanderson. Following the submission of the protocol, early approval was expected at the April meeting of the NIH Review Council. Miller was planning to hold a press conference as soon as he was officially notified of the plan's acceptance. At that time, 10 other centers would be selected to join his, based on letters sent to the NIH containing plans from the respective centers on how they would implement the protocol. The purpose of the press conference was two-fold: to announce this important step forward in medical research (and not so incidentally, give themselves a pat on the back), but also to prod the Food and Drug Administration into giving a "fast-track" approval for the drugs that would be used as soon as they demonstrated their benefits in the patient studies. Miller was fully confident that the study would be a tremendous clinical advance.

When he called Bergman into his office on a sunny day in mid-March, Bergman hoped Miller had found out about his snooping into the "missing-dog" issue so that he could finally unburden himself. But that was not the case. Bergman didn't—or couldn't—find the right moment to blurt out his concerns. Instead, Bergman listened to his chief's musings, content to play the role of sounding board that Miller had obviously envisioned for him that afternoon. From his new miniature CD player, a Christmas gift from his wife, a Bach concerto wafted delightfully through the room.

Miller leaned back in his chair and stared at the ceiling over his head. "The press conference could be important to our efforts in a variety of ways, some of them not obvious, because they're related to what I'm forced to term the politics of academic medicine. You saw some of that at our NCS meeting. Since perception is sometimes as important as reality, we must always be seen as an active research center. This attracts the brightest fellows, and because some of our funding comes from the state, the legislature is always looking for proof that its money is being used for worthy causes. So, the press conference will serve several purposes." The Bach concerto ended, and he moved his swivel chair to the side of the desk that his CD player was on to put in a new recording.

"I like bouncing ideas off of you," Miller said, smiling. "You've got a good head on your shoulders. In a few months you'll be a third-year fellow, and then we'll have to sit down and plan the next steps of your career. Your maturity and poise are heartening to see these days, so I hope you don't mind my asking your opinions on these matters. It's good to get a younger person's viewpoint. In some ways, I'm getting too old to always see the forest for the trees, or whatever that expression is." He laughed easily. Bergman decided it was not the right moment for him to unburden himself about Sanderson.

The press conference went off as planned. It was held in the main auditorium the week after the NIH officially approved the protocol. Ever the politician, Miller made sure the dean and chief of medicine were invited, though neither attended. Miller took it in stride. "They're already jealous enough; this won't help," he told Bergman. The announcement of the study received generous attention from the wire services, but the *New York Times*, Science Times section only carried a two-paragraph filler, and the news magazines ignored it completely, which was probably appropriate, since there were as yet no human results. What especially annoyed Bergman, however, was the increased attention Sanderson's animal work now received as an offshoot of the clinical trial. It also irked Douglas because, just as Jennifer had predicted, he wanted to know what Bergman had done to stop Sanderson. Douglas would end his fellowship in June and begin his new job in Boston on July 1st; he wanted this matter cleared up before he left town. When Bergman told him he had done nothing—even after his visit to O'Brien—Douglas became visibly upset.

"I thought I could trust you to handle this," he said, shaking his head. "I guess I misjudged you."

Embarrassed, Bergman could only promise to bring it to Miller's attention at the next opportunity.

"Forget it," Douglas muttered angrily. "I'll do it myself."

Before Bergman could attempt to argue him out of it, Douglas had stalked off. It was probably right, Bergman decided later in the day when he thought about it, that he had let Douglas down. Douglas was better off handling it directly.

Jennifer agreed when he told her about it that night. "It was his idea in the first place," she said, "so it's not out-of-place for him to be the one to bother the boss with it. Don't be so hard on yourself, Paul. You can't do *everything* well. You're only human."

She was right, Bergman knew, but somehow in those last few days of April, he had a sense of foreboding that this spring would bring more than pleasant weather and colorful flowers. Especially since next week the *New England Medical Review* was scheduled to publish Sanderson's latest article. Bergman knew Douglas was not going to let that event pass unnoticed.

CHAPTER

23

The first week in May arrived and the article in the *New England Medical Review* appeared as scheduled. It reported on Sanderson's most important study, one of those that he had presented in abstract form at the NCS meeting in Atlanta in January. The mechanism of fatal heart attacks was clearly demonstrated in these animal experiments, as was the suggested technique for correcting the problem with new drugs. The implication for humans was obvious, and the accompanying editorial praised the work effusively.

As was usual with clinically important lead articles in the *Review*, the media picked up the story and in order to interpret the results for a wider lay audience, embellished its importance considerably. But, by any standard, it was apparent something important had taken place in Miller's laboratory. Forewarned, Miller had prepared his own comments in such a way as to defuse criticism from PETA and other animal-rights groups. When interviewed, Miller stressed that, although the animals were awake and presumably suffered some discomfort when they had their heart attacks, it was clear that only in this way could the human situation be adequately replicated. (Ironically, it was Bergman's device that enabled Sanderson and O'Brien to do this maneuver, but again nothing was said about it.) Miller's tone was so sincere, and his approach to the issue so forthright, that he disarmed many potential adversaries before they were able to mount any attacks. Aside from some minor grumbling by a small university animal-rights group, the matter seemed a non-issue.

Before Miller could enjoy his triumph fully, Douglas paid him a visit. The next day Miller called Bergman into his office and related what had transpired during Douglas' visit. Miller's expression was one of puzzlement.

"I can't understand why Bill Douglas would think Sanderson's experiments were somehow tainted. I've heard his presentations and the data looked excellent. But Bill said he had told you about it, and you had agreed to look into it for him. Is this true?"

"Yes."

"Why didn't you tell me?"

"I first wanted to satisfy myself that there was really something wrong."

"And did you?"

"I think so."

"When was this?"

"In the last several weeks."

"I find it very hard to believe his work is fraudulent."

Bergman sighed heavily. "That was my reaction at first, but the more questions I asked . . ."

Miller's tone became angry. "This is very serious business, Paul. A lot of our efforts are tied into Sanderson's work. I hope you realize that?"

"I do."

He picked up the telephone and called the animal lab. "Charlie? Leo. Could you come up here for a few minutes? Thanks."

Neither of them said anything more until O'Brien came in.

"Hello, Leo."

"Take a seat, Charlie. I'm afraid there's some unpleasant business to discuss."

O'Brien sat opposite Bergman. "I thought the animal-rights people were lying low," he said.

"They are. This has nothing to do with them. Charlie, how closely have you been monitoring Sanderson's experiments?"

"Very closely. In fact, I'm often involved in them, personally."

"Have you ever seen him do anything incorrectly? I mean, cut corners, and falsify data?"

O'Brien looked at Bergman sharply. Now he knew why he had been summoned.

"I'm surprised at you, Bergman," O'Brien said, practically hissing at him. "I never thought you'd stoop this low."

"You knew about this?" Miller asked, surprised.

"Bergman came to me last month with his suspicions. I told him there was nothing to them, and I certainly wasn't going to bother you with them."

Miller shook his head and frowned. "I appreciate your concern, Charlie, but don't you think I should have been made aware ..."

"Only if there were something wrong, Leo," O'Brien interrupted him. "You're a great believer in civil liberties. Why impugn an innocent person unnecessarily? And believe me, there was nothing to it. Bergman's charges were very offbase."

"They weren't Paul's charges," Miller said.

"Whose ever charges. All I know is that Bergman was the one that came to see me."

Miller stood up and paced around the room. "You said you looked into it, Charlie. What exactly does that mean?"

"I met with Sanderson that night and went over his data books. Everything seemed in order as I suspected it would."

"Was Sanderson offended?"

"I didn't tell him someone had made charges against him. I just said I wanted to review all the data to refresh my memory. That was just before his first paper was published, and I told him I needed to be able to respond to any question that the paper might provoke. Scientific questions, not questions about false data and fraud. I never mentioned that word."

Bergman shivered. The word was finally spoken—the word Douglas and he had never uttered through all their conversations—the word that Miller had carefully avoided. Now it was out on the table. Fraud! A horrible word on a university campus.

Miller stopped his pacing. "So the extent of your check-up was to go over Sanderson's records?"

"Yes. What more was I supposed to do? Everything was in order. How many times do I have to repeat that?"

Miller ignored O'Brien's tone. "And the dog count? What about that?"

O'Brien leaped to his feet. "Dog count?" he yelled. "Leo, I've got better things to do than count the number of dogs we've sacrificed."

"Calm down, Charlie. I'm on your side, believe me. I have no desire to unfairly accuse Sanderson of anything. But, I've got to get to the bottom of this."

"Of what?" O'Brien snarled. "There isn't anything to get to the bottom of. I told you— I went over Sanderson's data with him. I'm satisfied."

Miller eyed him carefully. "I believe you, Charlie. Now satisfy me."

"How?"

Miller must have remembered something Douglas had told him at that point because he said, "Bring me the pressure tracing from the series of dogs that Sanderson reported this week in the *New England Medical Review.*"

"Fine. No problem."

"Do it now, please."

"Sure." He got up and left.

"I think Douglas is way off base, Paul. O'Brien runs a tight ship down there. He has too much at stake to approve shoddy reports."

That was true, Bergman knew.

"And Sanderson has done such good work for him," Miller continued. "He's taken a personal interest in his career. That's why Sanderson's been appointed to the faculty—on Charlie's recommendation. He would never go out on a limb for someone who was dishonest. I think Bill Douglas just got carried away."

"But the dog count? And the make-up experiments Sanderson's been grinding out?"

"I'm sure there's a good explanation for both."

The phone rang. O'Brien was calling from the dog lab. Miller listened grimly.

"Yes, Charlie, I understand. Tomorrow at the latest." He put down the receiver. "O'Brien can't find the pressure tracings. Sanderson must have taken them home with him. He'll have him bring them tomorrow."

Bergman said nothing. He didn't have to. Anyone who worked in the lab knew it was strictly against department policy to take any raw data out of the lab. Bergman could see the beginning doubts creep over Miller's hawk-like face; he knew the feeling well. It was the same feeling he had when he had initially finished with Eddy's log book.

That night, when he told Jennifer what was happening, she didn't seem too surprised. "There's some serious psychopathology out there," she said. "Dr. Sanderson may be in for some trouble."

"A case of the chickens coming home to roost?"

"You don't sound too displeased."

But actually, he was. Sanderson would not only bring down his own career, but conceivably he could damage O'Brien's and even Miller's. The collateral damage could be widespread. In fact, anyone connected to that animal lab—himself included—could be tarnished.

The next morning, Friday, ushered in one of those lovely warm May days that make life feel worthwhile. Plump, orange-breasted robins chirped happily, trees showed off their first green buds, and tulips stood majestically upright in celebration of their short but glorious lives.

This was the day Sanderson was to deliver his records and pressure tracings to O'Brien, who in turn would bring them to Miller's office. When O'Brien arrived, Miller sent for Bergman so that he could join them in what would be a very unpleasant task—reviewing a colleague's records to document cheating. They spread out Sanderson's data on Miller's work table and compared the material in his published article with the actual results.

The first discrepancy was obvious.

"He's reported the results in sixteen dogs," Miller said angrily, "but he's only given us seven records. What kind of fools does he take us for?"

O'Brien shrugged. "He knows he's short. He told me he would look throughout his apartment over the weekend for the other tracings."

"What did he say when you reminded him of the department policy about not taking material home?"

"He said he forgot."

"Did you believe him?"

"I wanted to," O'Brien said evenly, "but I couldn't." Verbalizing this admission seemed to upset O'Brien, because he lost his composure and began cursing. "That fucking bastard," he said, over and over, until Miller told him to stop.

"Maybe he'll find the rest," Miller said softly. Now he turned to Bergman. "What do you think of the article?"

"It's very good," he replied. "Maybe too good."

"What do you mean?" Miller asked sharply.

"Look at Figure 2." This figure was a plot of the data points over time. Each of the points fell on a line of identity that ran from the lower left-hand corner of the graph to the upper right-hand corner. "There's very little scatter to these points. The correlation coefficient is 0.98. I've never seen one so close to 1.0; have you?"

Miller studied the figure. Scientists realized that 1.0—the perfect coefficient—was an impossibility in any experimental study, but in Miller's extensive experience, so was 0.98. Miller's face fell. "We should have picked this up earlier, Charlie. Paul's right, it's *too* good."

It was now O'Brien's turn to study the graph. "I remember in his earlier papers the correlation coefficients were more realistic, 0.82 and so forth. There was more scatter. I guess I just assumed his technique was getting better."

"You didn't check the points on the graph against the raw data?"

"No."

"Why don't you do it now?" He thrust across one of the pressure tracings and watched while O'Brien copied down the data points and checked them against Sanderson's log. The points in the log book formed the basis for the graph.

After a few minutes, O'Brien looked up. "The raw data doesn't agree with what's in the log book. The numbers have been improved." He said it matter-of-factly, but Bergman knew by his eyes that he had been hurt, deeply hurt, by what he had found.

Miller held his head in his hands. "So we have false data entries, as well as totally fabricated components."

"Only in this series of experiments," O'Brien reminded him. "We don't know if it applies to his earlier work."

Miller turned to Bergman. "What did you tell me about the earlier studies? That he added cases in an abbreviated manner?"

"After Dr. O'Brien talked to him about making sure his records were in order, Sanderson ran through a series of sham experiments to obtain raw data to make up for the animals he had never used. He didn't seem to care how half-assed they were or who saw him putting false dates on the pressure tracings."

"Did Eddy help him with those experiments?" O'Brien asked.

"Yes, but he had no knowledge of what Sanderson was up to because Sanderson did it right after the other abstracts were presented."

Miller rubbed his forehead. "If what you suspect is correct, Paul, Sanderson should be in the lab right now, manufacturing data that he can then claim to be the missing records he "found" at home. Charlie, why don't you call Eddy and see if anything is going on."

O'Brien did as he was told. "Eddy, anything on in Room 1? Oh, really. Since what time this morning? Okay, thanks." When he put down the phone, O'Brien looked like a beaten man. "Sanderson's been there since 6 a.m. Eddy's not sure what the protocol is, but he says Sanderson's cranking out data like a man possessed."

"Must be one scared young man," Miller said.

"Not according to Eddy. He's whistling one song after another. Seems happy as a lark." O'Brien shook his head in disbelief. "I think it's time to talk to Eddy. I told him to make some excuse and slip into my office."

After O'Brien left, Bergman remained in Miller's office for several minutes. Miller said nothing during that time, his thoughts obviously elsewhere. Bergman felt awkward, as if he were intruding on Miller's inner sanctum, and got up to leave.

"Say nothing about this to anyone," Miller told him. "I plan on using the weekend to come up with a way out of this mess, if I can." His tone was not optimistic.

Bergman went down to the animal lab. O'Brien was still waiting for Eddy to show up. It was not especially warm in the lab, but O'Brien was sweating profusely.

"I'm scared," O'Brien said. "I'm scared that you are right and Sanderson's going to ruin us all. I can just see the look on Wentworth's face when he hears about this."

"Why are you so sure Wentworth and the dean won't back Leo up?

"I know Wentworth used to date Arlene when he and Leo were house officers. Leo stole her away and Wentworth never forgave him. He hates her now and he's jealous of Leo and that makes him hate Leo even more. Plain and simple."

Bergman now realized how much danger Miller was in. "The problem is that Wentworth is now Leo's boss, and that's a bad spot for Leo to be in," O'Brien went on. "Wentworth doesn't miss an opportunity to poison the well about Leo with the dean who's an old buddy of his. Of course, Leo helps. He's such a stubborn bastard. He was going to fine me a couple of times for showing up drunk at conferences, but Arlene wouldn't let him. She even stood up for me when I made an ass of myself at one of Wentworth's parties. What a classy lady. And now I've given Wentworth a chance to get back at her and Leo. Shit. That's what I feel like—shit." He glared at Bergman. "Go on, get out of here. Haven't you caused enough trouble? I'll handle Eddy. Get out of here."

CHAPTER

24

The weekend turned out to be summery. The newlyweds spent it outdoors as much as possible, hiking and picnicking in the hills overlooking the town. A large wildlife refuge occupied almost 30 acres and afforded them as much seclusion as one could reasonably ask for. Bergman lay on the grass, his head on Jennifer's lap, and contemplated the cloudless blue sky . "What are you thinking about?" Jennifer asked.

"What I usually think about these days. Eric G. Sanderson, III and what makes him tick."

"I'm sure that's what your boss is also contemplating."

"He's got more on his mind than just that. He has to figure out a solution. I think he's secretly praying that all those missing lab reports will turn up and spare him any further grief."

"Is that likely?"

"In my opinion? As likely as a snowstorm in May."

"Well, you know they did have a snowstorm here on this day a few years ago?"

"You're joking."

"No. I'm not. It was the famous Mother's Day snowstorm."

"Oh, my God! Is today Mother's Day?"

"Second Sunday in May."

"I forgot to send my mother a card. Why didn't you remind me?"

Jennifer laughed. "I never send cards. I always call. It's better, more personal. We'll both call tonight. Anyway, we have something important to tell the both of them."

"We do?"

"Yes, we do." She reached over and kissed him on the lips.

"What do we have to tell them?" Bergman asked.

"Well, considering your intelligence and considering what day today is, let's see if you can put two and two together."

"Holy cow, you're pregnant!"

She beamed delightedly. "You're right ... and I'm due in the middle of October. What do you think of that, Dad?"

Dad. He liked the way that sounded. He couldn't think of a better day—or setting—to find out he was a father-to-be.

That Monday, after making rounds with Dr. Goldberg on the Consult Service, Bergman went to Miller's office to see if he needed any help going over the latest installment of animal data from Sanderson's experiments. By the time he reached the reception area, Miller's secretary had already gone off to lunch. He knocked firmly on the door to Miller's private office.

Several minutes later—and still no answer to his knock—he made up his mind to leave. Just as he was about to, the door opened slowly and Miller beckoned him to come in. His face had lost its normal pink tones and was almost ashen. He looked ill. Bergman wondered if he had the flu.

"Sit down," Miller insisted.

"I came to offer my help again," Bergman said.

"Help?"

"Help in going over the Sanderson experiments. I expected Dr. O'Brien to be here also."

Miller looked at Bergman strangely. "You haven't heard, then?"

"Heard what?" Bergman asked.

"O'Brien came to see me at nine o'clock on the dot, as promised. But he didn't have any data with him."

"Sanderson couldn't find more records? Or did he admit he never had any?"

Miller smiled wanly. "I can't answer those questions and neither can Charlie. When he went to Sanderson's apartment earlier this morning—as suggested by Sanderson on Friday afternoon—no one answered the door. According to the landlord, Sanderson left a check for this month's rent and said he would be away for awhile. His lease is up at the end of June anyway, so Charlie figured the landlord would use the security deposit to cover June if he doesn't come back."

"I don't understand," Bergman said, genuinely bewildered at the sudden turn of events. "What do you mean, if he doesn't come back?"

"I think he's gone, Paul, G-O-N-E. And for good."

Miller stared at the wall behind Bergman. "Running away like this is as good an admission of guilt as signing a confession would be. It puts all of us in an awful situation, especially me. Quite frankly, I'm a little dazed by it, and I'm going to need some time to compose my thoughts. You can do me one favor, though."

"Sure. Anything."

"See if the other fellows know where he might have gone. I would still like to have a least one face-to-face confrontation with him."

Bergman said he would do what he could. Walking aimlessly through the bustling corridors of the hospital, he pondered long and hard whom to approach first. The only thing that was not clear—and what he had neglected to ask Miller about—was whether anyone else besides O'Brien, Miller, and himself knew about Sanderson's flight. Obviously, his line of questioning would be different depending on that bit of information. As luck would have it, the first person from the Cardiology Division that he saw was Gus Adopolous. Gus was always up on the latest gossip; if word was out that Sanderson was in trouble, he would have heard about it.

"Gus, what rotation are you on this month?"

"Back on the CCU. My last month with Miller. In June, I start to pack it all in." Adopolous would be joining a four man private-practice group in Ohio on July 1st.

"I'm heading your way," Bergman said. "I'll keep you company for a few minutes."

They walked down the corridor together while Gus chatted about his wife's pleasure at leaving the northeast. "It will be sort of sad when this group breaks up though," Gus was saying. "Barnes is going back to LA, and I think Douglas will be in Boston. We've grown pretty close over the last two years. Even the guys who were a year ahead of us are a real good bunch." Finally, Bergman saw his opening.

"That reminds me," Bergman interjected. "Have you seen Sanderson lately?"

Adopolous replied without hesitation and Bergman knew the word was definitely not out. "I saw him at the echo conference last week, but not since. He barely said hello, which of course, is not unusual. Come to think of it, he's the exception to the rule, the one rotten apple in the whole barrel. At least as far as I'm concerned."

"But where is he now?"

"Damned if I know. Probably took off with Vicki, that cute redhead from the CCU."

Exactly. Bergman could have kicked himself for not thinking of that himself. When the automatic doors to the CCU swung open, Adopolous gave him a wave and Bergman went off to the fellows' room. He meandered over to the nurses' station.

Luckily, Vicki was on duty, writing notes in a patient's chart. "Hi," he began. She looked up with two of the most beautiful blue eyes he'd ever seen.

"Morning, Dr. Bergman."

"Good morning. Vicki, I'm looking for Eric. Have you seen him around?"

She frowned. "Sorry, but I can't help you. Dr. Sanderson and I are no longer on speaking terms."

"Oh, I'm sorry to hear that."

"Well, don't be. He turned out to be as big a creep as my friend warned me he would be. One-hundred eighty pounds of pure ego. If you'll excuse me, I really don't want to talk about it." She went back to her chart.

So apparently she didn't know Sanderson had taken off, much less where. Bergman called Miller's office and told him the well was dry.

"Could you come out to my house tonight at eight? Miller asked. "I want to brainstorm with you and O'Brien, and there just isn't time during the day."

Bergman agreed and rejoined his ward team for cardiology consults. The day went quickly and, after a fast supper with Jennifer at their apartment, he set out for Miller's home in the suburbs. In mid-May, his house presented a slightly different picture than it had when Bergman had first visited it on that September day almost two years earlier. Because the lush growth of summer was yet to come, the house was completely visible to him from the roadside, even before he entered the driveway. Arlene must have been busy planting impatiens over the weekend since the tiny plants seemed to be everywhere, arranged in bunches of whites, reds, and purples, still in tight, protective ranks, not yet ready to expand and spread as they would in one or two month's time.

A symphonic piece Bergman was not familiar with (it sounded too modern for Miller's taste) was playing on his stereo speakers. Miller was standing in his study, hands thrust into his pockets, contemplating his bookshelf. He did not look like a man with much on his mind.

"Come in, Paul, and sit down. O'Brien's not here yet."

Bergman sat in one of the comfortable leather armchairs by the fireplace.

"I don't recognize the music," he said.

"You think I only play Bach, don't you?" Miller said smiling.

"Not necessarily, but I do know you prefer anything baroque."

Miller took a cassette from a box and inserted it into his tape deck. "Tonight I'm trying to stay in the 20th century. But that piece doesn't quite have what I'm looking for, which is a sense of wistfulness, a nostalgia for times gone by, simpler times."

As if on cue, the music now emanating from the speakers was a big band sound from the forties.

"This song greeted me in 1945 when I returned to the States from the POW camp in the Philippines. Boy, was I glad to leave that place."

As the voice of the nineteen-year-old Doris Day picked up the refrain of *Sentimental Journey*, a big smile broke out on Leo Miller's face, and he actually started to sing along. "Gonna take a sentimental journey, journey back home ..." The words he didn't know he hummed along. Hands still in his pockets, he swayed gently to the music. It was a side of Miller, Bergman had never seen before. Arlene must have heard the change in music as well, because she started singing from one of the other rooms. In a few seconds, she had joined them in the study, and Miller was soon leading her around the room in a fox-trot. They were a graceful duo as they maneuvered their way around the furniture, never taking their eyes off each other. Bergman felt like an intruder and edged toward the door.

Miller saw what Bergman was doing and motioned for him to stand still. "Not so fast, my friend; this little touch of sentimentality is rapidly coming to an end. Then the wake will resume."

"Leo! Stop talking like that!" Arlene's voice was insistent. "You're making a mountain out of a mole hill."

The song was over and so was the dancing. Miller turned off the tape deck. Arlene smoothed her dress and gave him a big smile. "I hope you and Jennifer are still dancing like that when your thirtieth anniversary rolls around."

"That presumes a lot of things, dear," Miller growled, "not the least is that they can dance like that now. Not many young people are into ballroom style dancing."

"It's all right, Mrs. Miller," Bergman assured her. "At least on that score we qualify."

"Now, all they have to do is stay together for thirty years," Miller said, laughing.

The mood was so light and pleasant, Bergman almost forgot why he was there, but the doorbell brought them all back to reality. Arlene excused herself.

O'Brien looked tired. He sank immediately onto the sofa and rubbed his eyes. "I hope this isn't going to be long, Leo. I've had a rough day."

Miller shrugged. "We'll exchange ideas, maybe come up with some things to do, then break up. It shouldn't be that difficult. I appreciate your helping out, Charlie, I really do."

O'Brien nodded and then gestured at Bergman. "Is it really necessary for him to sit in on this?"

"I would think so," Miller said. "Paul's been trying to warn us about Sanderson for some time. Now that events have borne him out, he may be able to help us extricate ourselves from this mess. And don't kid yourself, Charlie, we are in a mess."

O'Brien grunted. "I know, I know."

Miller paced around the room alternately eyeing each of them. "Anytime either of you wants to say something, just interrupt me. But it seems to me there are several things we have to do, and we have to do them quickly. By the way, the first thing to do is establish if the conclusions of Sanderson's published reports are consistent with actual data. If so, that will soften the impact when we retract those papers."

"If you prove the conclusions correct, why do you have to withdraw the papers?" Bergman asked.

"Because they were purposefully misrepresented. We really have no choice."

"To do over the published papers," O'Brien said, "I'm going to need some help. More than just Douglas, whom I'm assuming will help. What about you, Bergman?"

"Whatever it takes, I'm with you."

"That a promise? It's going to mean nights and weekends."

"A promise. But I suggest you talk to Bill Douglas personally. He needs a little stroking at this point."

Miller nodded his assent.

"So it was Douglas who was wise to Sanderson," O'Brien mused. "Ahead of all of us, I guess. But what do we tell the other fellows and the faculty? That Sanderson's decided not to join our staff in July? That he's taken another job offer?"

Miller shook his head. "We just tell whoever asks that he's disappeared, and we don't know why. This is the time of year when there's always confusion about who left early, etc. The real problem will come on July 1st, when he's supposed to become an Attending. That's when the administration will be asking questions about the missing faculty member. A fellow can be missed, but not a new assistant professor."

O'Brien nodded. "So we have about six weeks to redo his experiments before too many questions are asked?"

"Right."

"When are you going to inform the journals?" Bergman asked.

"Early in July, when the duplication studies are done."

"Same thing for the department chairman and the dean?"

Miller stopped pacing. This was the crucial issue—when to inform his superiors of the suspected fraud. It would be one thing if they were friends of his, but neither of the two was in that category. "I've been giving that a lot of thought. They're going to jump all over me for this one, no question about it. It seems to me I better know as much of the facts as possible before I open my mouth."

O'Brien disagreed. "Tell them now! Explain that you're going to look into the matter. The longer you wait, the more it looks like you're trying to cover up."

"What do you think, Paul?" Miller asked.

"I agree with Dr. O'Brien."

For the first time Bergman saw Miller's stubborn side. "I thank you both for your candor, but on this point, I've made up my mind. I can't face them without knowing the outcome of the re-do studies."

For the next half-hour they discussed in detail the way the experiments would proceed. Finally, O'Brien's weariness brought the meeting to a close. He departed quickly. Before leaving, Bergman had one last question to ask Miller.

"I still don't understand why Sanderson did it. He had the world at his feet. He didn't have to cheat."

Miller nodded. "There aren't any easy answers to that question. I certainly don't have any. It's a question your wife and her psychology colleagues could probably answer better. He must be a very troubled young man."

Shaking his head, whether in sympathy or disgust (Bergman couldn't be sure), Miller bade him goodnight and started thumbing through his cassette collection again. Bergman had a feeling he was looking for some more upbeat selections from 1945.

CHAPTER

25

Bergman remembered Miller's words when he arrived home that evening. After dinner, he sat Jennifer down on the sofa in the living room and posed the same question to her that he asked himself earlier in the afternoon.

"What made Sanderson do this?"

"First of all, why do you thing he's so unique? Isn't academic cheating rather common?"

"So typical of a shrink," he said, "answering one question by asking another." After several minutes enduring her bemused stare, he cleared his throat and finally replied to her question.

"I wouldn't say academic fraud is common. In fact, it's very unusual, but, yes, it does occur. Is there any thread that connects one scandal to another? I don't know. No two are really the same."

"But don't they fall into certain categories? I mean this one seems different from the one I read about in the newspapers last year. I think a professor had plagiarized articles in writing a paper and was turned in by a graduate student; the professor was fired, or something like that."

He remembered the case. It wasn't exactly as Jennifer had recalled it, but the facts were similar. "That was really bizarre," he said. "The professor was writing a review article. It wasn't meant to be an original article. He had over one hundred references, but apparently one or two sentences were almost identical to those in an article he hadn't referenced. On that bit of esoterica, his career was endangered. Maybe university politics also played a role; you can never tell. There was also the case of the respected cancer researcher who falsified data to conform to his theories. Painting splotches on the back of rats, that sort of thing. Much, much more serious fraud. But you're right, in a sense. These things do fall into certain patterns. Usually a young research assistant misrepresents data, like Sanderson did."

"Young investigators want to move up the ladder quickly. They take a shortcut. That sounds like Sanderson's motives."

He shook his head. "It's too pat an answer. He didn't have to do this. He could have presented two or three papers at a meeting instead of six and would have been considered just as successful."

"Inner demons?"

"Probably. I just feel something's wrong with him," he said, remembering Miller's diagnosis of a very troubled young man."

Jennifer agreed. "The key is to find out if this is the first time he's done something like this. Because if it isn't, it shows a pattern of behavior that has been abnormal for some time."

"You know, that's an excellent point, but I really don't know the answer. As far as I know, this is the first example of this type of behavior, but it's a fascinating thought."

"Now you know why you married me. Good insight."

They both laughed at that, but in a way she was right. What was wrong with having a wife with both brains and beauty?

The next several weeks were unbelievably hectic. By day, Bergman worked hard, very hard, on the consult service seeing patients with Dr. Goldberg. By night, he worked with Charlie O'Brien and Bill Douglas. Douglas was not at all annoyed at the need for the extra work. Bergman would like to say they sailed through the experiments, but that would be a gross exaggeration—plowed through them was more like it. Ironically, the results clearly confirmed the conclusions that Sanderson had reached. It was soon obvious to all of them that Sanderson's initial impressions were correct, and that there had been no need at all for the cheating. What demons possessed Sanderson? Bergman couldn't say. He didn't know. O'Brien and Douglas were as puzzled as he was. Could it be that Sanderson was just lazy; he didn't want to do all the work necessary for a complete study. But knowing Sanderson as they did—however limited their insight into his psyche— they knew that answer was not sufficient. A truly lazy person would never spend the hours he did working in an oppressively hot animal laboratory during those unbearable days last July and August.

Towards the middle of June, they presented Miller with enough data for him to feel comfortable with Sanderson's conclusions, the misrepresentation of the numbers of dogs used notwithstanding.

Recalculation of the statistics now provided more reasonable numbers for standard errors, regression coefficients, etc. They had thoroughly "cleaned up" his data. The cost to the laboratory was not insignificant. Almost seventy-five dogs had been ordered under urgent conditions, which doubled the normal price per dog to about 400 dollars.

They were all exhausted, but felt it was worth it. O'Brien seemed genuinely impressed by Bergman's and Douglas' efforts, especially since Bergman had left his newly pregnant, and consistently nauseated, wife for long stretches to help O'Brien and Douglas. Douglas prepared to leave for his internship knowing he had not only uncovered cheating, but had also saved the reputation of his mentor—or so he thought. The next logical step was to inform the department chairman and dean of what had happened and to write to the journals involved so that retractions could be printed; but a retraction with the important caveat that repeat experiments had now been completed verifying the original conclusions.

From what Bergman gathered later on, Miller had planned to do this as quickly as possible. He received the data from them on Monday, and his secretary had arranged a meeting as soon as Smiley and Wentworth had free time, which turned out to be Wednesday morning.

Unfortunately, Wednesday was too late. On Tuesday afternoon, the hospital was treated to the unusual sight of two gray-and-blue state police cruisers parked at the main entrance to the hospital. Police cars in the emergency entrance were, of course, a common sight, but at the front door? Bergman asked the receptionist at the main information desk in the lobby if she knew what was going on. She certainly did.

"Haven't you heard, doctor? I thought the whole hospital knew."

"Knew what?"

"Why, one of your colleagues is missing, maybe even murdered." She pronounced the last word slowly and forcefully.

"One of our doctors?" Bergman was incredulous. "But this neighborhood's still one of the safest in the city."

"Oh, he wasn't killed here," she said matter-of-factly. "No one knows for sure. Anyway, that's the rumor."

"Do you know who it was?"

"A cardiology fellow. Dr. Sanderson."

"Oh, my God!" Bergman's face froze in dismay. He didn't know who he was more sorry for, Sanderson or Miller. Now the fat was in the fire for sure.

Bergman made his way through the crowded lobby to one of the intra-hospital wall phones. Leo Miller's secretary wouldn't connect him.

"He's in conference."

"Look, it's Paul Bergman. I've got to let him know the police are here. Dr. Sanderson's missing and may be dead."

"He knows that, Dr. Bergman. The police are in his office. They've been there for about an hour already. Why don't you come around in about half an hour, and I'll squeeze you into his schedule."

"Okay."

When he finally got to see him, Miller was distraught as he told Bergman what the police had said.

"Sanderson's mother filed a missing person's report when she hadn't heard from him for a while. The police went to his rooms, found them empty, with the contents of the room in disarray, possibly a burglary. No body found."

"So maybe he's not dead?"

"Maybe, maybe not. Unfortunately, he had been scribbling notes in his bed when he was still there, and my name's all over them. I don't think the police seriously consider me a suspect in any crime, but I'm not sure. I'm going to need a lawyer, since I do have motive given Sanderson's history of cheating in my lab."

"Could have been a bungled burglary. That area's notorious for break-ins. Do they think the burglars kidnapped him? That's weird."

"I agree, but according to the police it could have been made to look like a burglary. I had to tell them about Sanderson's problems here, so naturally they wondered if I was trying to shut him up. I suppose that's what policemen are supposed to do, explore all sorts of theories. Now I have to explain all of this to Wentworth and the dean before they hear about it from others. In hindsight, you and O'Brien were right. I should have told them about the cheating right from the start." He sighed in disgust.

"Anything I can do to help?"

He shook his head. "I appreciate the offer, but I can't think of anything at the moment. I feel like a mountain has fallen on me. Maybe when I'm more composed, I'll think of something." He paused and rubbed his temples. "There are tough times ahead, very tough times.

CHAPTER

26

Rumors of Sanderson's disappearance swept through the hospital. In his three years there as cardiology fellow, he had been a familiar face on the wards, in the cafeteria, and at various house-staff social events. As a result, many hospital personnel, both physicians and non-physicians, had become acquainted with him. Also, contributing to the disbelief and shock at news of his possible abduction and death, was the aura of mystery that now surrounded his last few weeks. Why hadn't he been seen during the month of June? Only a handful of the staff really knew what was going on, and, in the absence of the truth, rumors began to circulate that he had a mental breakdown, probably due to overwork. He was known to be obsessed with his research; he had probably "stressed out" trying to accomplish too much. These thoughts were especially prevalent among the cardiology fellows and staff.

When Adopolous asked Bergman for his opinion, Bergman just shrugged his shoulders. What could he say without jeopardizing Miller? He knew too much and would have to wait for Miller to make some statement before opening his own mouth—except, of course, to Jennifer.

Lying in bed that night, with the windows wide open, and the never ending purr of traffic from the not-too-distant highway in the background, they talked about the tragedy that seemed to have befallen Sanderson. To have one's academic career ruined was one thing, but possibly to be killed because of it was another. Jennifer had little to add. The day's events had stunned her as much as the people at the hospital.

"I must admit I never liked him much from the first time I met him. I think he'd step on his grandmother if it would help his advancement, but even still..."

"Yeah, I know what you mean. I even feel a little guilty."

"Don't be ridiculous!"

"Still . . ."

"I'm more concerned with the effect on Leo Miller."

"The best clue to that will be in the morning, when Miller finally meets with the department chairman and the dean, Jack Smiley." He started to explain more but Jennifer was already asleep.

It was a meeting Bergman had no intention of attending, but to his surprise, he was called into Miller's office shortly before noon. O'Brien was already there.

When Wentworth and the dean arrived shortly thereafter, they were not pleased to see O'Brien and Bergman.

"Are you sure you want them to sit in on this, Leo?" Wentworth asked.

"You'll see in a minute how important a help they've been."

"A help?" the dean said derisively. "You've got yourself in one hell of a fix, and you talk about the help you received? You've really got balls, Leo."

Miller's eyebrows arched. He looked as if he was ready to reply but must have thought better of it, because he said nothing. Finally, Wentworth motioned with a wagging finger that they were waiting to hear something from Miller. "You called the meeting, Leo. What do you have to say?"

"Not only did I call the meeting, Harrison, but I arranged it last week, before Sanderson's disappearance. In fact, if you two had been more accommodating with your time, we probably could have met before this tragic event occurred."

"Maybe if you had told us how important it was, we could have accommodated you, as you put it." The dean's tone was as cold as it had been during his previous comment.

"Perhaps I should have," Miller conceded, "but that's water under the bridge now."

"Could we get on with this?" Wentworth snapped.

Miller stared at his boss with undisguised contempt. "That's what I'm trying to do. About six weeks ago, Paul Bergman," here he nodded in Bergman's direction, "came to me with reports of possible falsification of data during animal experiments conducted by Sanderson in Charlie O'Brien's laboratory. He had previously gone to Dr. O'Brien with his story, which he'd gotten from Bill Douglas, another second-year fellow working with Sanderson. Charlie had looked into the charges, but he had decided there was no proof they were true. However, when Bergman came to me with more evidence, I had O'Brien put pressure on Sanderson to produce the raw data so as to more definitely refute the charges. Sanderson promised to bring the missing files over the weekend, but then he disappeared."

"How long ago was this?" the dean asked.

"The end of May."

"Why didn't you tell me about it then?" Wentworth asked.

"I should have, Harrison, but my first reaction was of shock. I couldn't believe falsified data had been published from my unit, so I told O'Brien to repeat the missing experiments to make sure the conclusions were still valid, even thought the original number of cases were falsely reported."

The dean interrupted. "You mean Sanderson experimented on three or four animals and reported results for a dozen or so?

"More or less. He also fudged the studies to make the conclusions as striking as possible."

"What was the result of the repeat studies?" Wentworth asked.

"Charlie got Paul Bergman and Bill Douglas to help him. They worked like beavers on nights and weekends and finished duplicating all the published studies last week. All the original conclusions were valid, even with the corrections in the revised statistics. That's when I called your office to make this appointment. And of course, yesterday I learned—as you did—that Sanderson is now officially listed as a missing person."

"When the police told us that bit of news," the dean said curtly, "we didn't even realize he'd been missing. You can imagine how embarrassed the medical-school administration was."

"Not to mention the department," Wentworth added.

"I apologize for that. It was bad judgment on my part."

"We'll get to that later," the dean said, "but first, I have a question for Dr. O'Brien."

The dean turned his gaze on the helpless O'Brien, who seemed to cringe in anticipation of the forthcoming assault.

"How can you account for this apparent falsification of data going on under your very nose?"

O'Brien mumbled something unintelligible.

"Speak up," the dean said sharply.

"I can't explain it," O'Brien said.

"Obviously, you trusted Sanderson too much. You didn't exercise proper supervision of your research laboratory, Dr. O'Brien. You must bear a large share of the responsibility for this fiasco."

O'Brien nodded slowly.

The dean turned back to Miller. "Well, Leo, how do you explain it?"

"We made a mistake with Sanderson; his initial work—which was thoroughly checked, by the way—was so good, we gave him too much leeway with his later studies."

"The "golden boy" syndrome?"

"I guess so."

The dean persisted, leaning forward to ask the next question.

"How many papers did he publish during his three years with you?"

Miller thought for a moment. "Three published, three in press, plus 12 abstracts presented: four in his second year and eight this year."

"And, of course, your name is on all of them?"

"Yes."

"What are you going to do about them?" Wentworth asked.

"My name is on them, so I'll retract them. I'll retract all of them. That's why I wanted to know if the conclusions were valid or not. I wanted to be able to publish a retraction while, hopefully, stating that the conclusions were still valid."

"You took a chance by waiting," Wentworth said. "I don't think it showed good judgment. Now, with Sanderson's disappearance and your name on what may have been deathbed notes, you're also under police investigation."

"But not as a serious suspect," Miller added. "I can assure you, I had nothing to do with his disappearance."

The dean cleared his throat. "Until you're officially cleared, it just adds to the burden on this medical center."

"It's a mess," Wentworth said in disgust. "Now, either this man Sanderson was some kind of nut, or the competitive atmosphere of your laboratory drove him to cheating. I tend to think the latter, and I have to act accordingly."

"What are you going to do, Harrison?" the dean asked.

"For starters, I think Dr. O'Brien has to be officially reprimanded and Dr. Miller's behavior questioned."

"I'll be ruined," O'Brien objected loudly.

"You brought it on yourself," Wentworth replied. "We have to show a strong internal investigation or the NIH will come in and blast us. All of your lab research is NIH-funded, isn't it?"

O'Brien nodded glumly.

"Last year the NIH came down very hard on Harvard, because their internal investigation of a surgical research scandal was nothing more than a whitewash. We can't allow that to happen here," Wentworth said sharply, with the most animation Bergman had ever seen in the man. "We will not deal with this business as if it were an everyday occurrence. I'm telling you quite candidly, Leo, this is a disgrace. The original malfeasance was bad enough. It shows a poorly-run unit, in my opinion. And the cover-up was just as bad."

"There was no cover-up," Miller insisted.

"Call it what you will. It smells rotten in any case. I'll have more to say to you in a few days." With that, he got up to leave and the dean joined him.

When they were gone, O'Brien and Miller exchanged glum looks.

"I'll have to quit," O'Brien said "or it will be your head they'll be after."

"I have a notion they'll be after it anyway," Miller replied.

CHAPTER

27

When Miller came home that evening, Arlene was on her third scotch-and-soda. She barely looked up when the front door shut behind him. "Don't bother lecturing me. I know what I'm doing."

"What are you doing?"

"I'm having a drink for old times' sake, if you must know." The words were slurred.

Miller gently took the glass from her hand and sat down on the couch beside her. With his arm around her, he kissed her forehead.

"Believe it or not, it's going to be okay," he said.

"No, it's not."

"I made a mistake. I was distracted, didn't keep close enough tabs on the lab; it won't happen again."

"Doesn't matter. Too late. That son of a bitch has knifed you—in the back—that fraud, that cheat. God, how I hate him!"

Miller said nothing.

"I could have killed him with my bare hands," she went on. "But I guess someone beat me to it. It wasn't you, was it Leo? You didn't kill the bastard?"

"No, but I should have caught his fraud. I'm not as quick as I used to be, I'm off my game, Arlene, and the chickens have come home to roost."

"I love you, Leo."

"I know, sweetheart."

"They're going to crucify you, aren't they?"

"They will try, that's for sure."

"Don't let them, Leo, for God's sake, don't let them. Be strong."

CHAPTER

28

The next day, the local tabloid picked up the story of Sanderson's disappearance and ran it on page two under a picture of Sanderson in his hospital whites. The police reported no clues as to his whereabouts or whether he was alive or dead. Miller's name was not mentioned, nor was there any mention of Sanderson's not reporting for work for the last four weeks or so. How long the press would remain ignorant of the latter item, Bergman was afraid to guess.

The effect of the news story on the staff of the cardiology section was devastating, even more so than it had been the day before, when the rumors first surfaced. One of their colleagues had possibly been killed, perhaps in an especially brutal way. After the initial shock wore off, the same questions were raised over and over by both fellows and attendings: Why hadn't anyone seen him around the hospital in weeks?

Later in the day, Miller finally put out a brief memo informing everyone that Sanderson had been missing ever since an investigation into alleged falsification of data in the animal laboratory had begun. Miller explained to Bergman that since he was also writing to the medical journals retracting Sanderson's articles and the dean's office was contemplating disciplinary action, there didn't seem much point in keeping the matter quiet any longer. Although Miller did not mention any theories about a deterioration in Sanderson's mental health, the implication was clear.

In his laboratory O'Brien was besieged with calls, but he refused to answer any of them. Eddy fended them off as best he could. Douglas and Bergman also kept a low profile and, in fact, Douglas was already preparing to leave in a few days to move into Boston to head a cardiac clinic in the Roxbury area. He seemed genuinely sorry for Sanderson, especially sorry that the fall from grace may have led to his death, but he also seemed relieved to be leaving town during this unsettling time.

"There's a lot of shit that's going to hit the fan around this place," he said, when Bergman went to his place to say goodbye on June 28th.

"You mean with O'Brien?"

"I mean with both of them." Bergman didn't have to ask who the other person was.

"Hey," Douglas added, "if you need my help again, let me know. Boston's not so far, you know."

They shook hands warmly.

For the next several weeks, the entire hospital staff was caught up in the yearly ritual of welcoming the new interns, residents, and of course, cardiology fellows. Though a busy period, it was actually a merciful respite from the repercussions of the "Sanderson affair," as the cheating scandal and subsequent disappearance came to be known. Bergman hardly had a private minute with Miller, but that was not a great loss for either of them. Miller had his work to do and Bergman had his. Most importantly, nothing more had emanated from the dean's office, and the police investigation cleared Miller of any involvement in Sanderson's disappearance. O'Brien had begun the lengthy process of looking for another job, sending his curriculum vitae out to medical schools and hospitals across the country. Somewhere there would be a cardiology division or physiology department looking for an experienced person to run their animal-research laboratory. Meanwhile, the journals had responded promptly to Miller's retraction request and were preparing short notices for the September issue (the August issues were already in press).

The advent of summer meant that Jennifer and Paul could get away to one of the lakes not far from the city on those weekends that he wasn't on call. Those were precious times for the two of them. She had gotten over her nausea and vomiting spells and was tolerating the early stages of her pregnancy as well as possible. Her cheeks seemed to have a permanent blush to them, as if she were applying rouge three or four times a day. They enjoyed the warm days of July and August and especially the trips to the lake. It was a time of closeness, of waiting for the unknown: their new child. Bergman particularly liked lying next to her on the old army blanket that they used to cover the sand on the beach. Stroking her hair while the sun burned down on the both of them, nuzzling her neck, feeling the bulge of the enlarged uterus beneath her bathing suit—all these things drew them even closer together.

But, of course, this was just the lull before the final storm. The furies that had been gathering ever since word of Sanderson's disappearance had reached the halls of the hospital now burst forth unrestrained. In early September, the dean suddenly announced that the medical-center authorities were going to conduct a full investigation into the cheating scandal and its cover-up. The announcement actually used the word "cover-up." By doing so, of course, there was no longer any pretense of who the target would be. Miller called Bergman the day after the dean's announcement—a Friday—and asked if he would mind spending some time with him over the weekend. He sounded awful. Bergman told him that he would make time on Saturday, but he wanted to spend Sunday with Jennifer. Miller didn't protest, but instead seemed grateful for any time he could spare for him.

"Be kind. If nothing else, be kind," Jennifer said the next day before he set out. It was good advice.

The Miller home in the midst of a surprising September heat wave was a cool refuge, but Miller could not be pent up indoors. There was too much electric energy to be dispensed. Even as he talked, he had to walk, to be constantly in motion. At first it was just chatter. He joked a bit about his garden, then headed off on a trail behind his house that led to the nature conservatory. Bergman tagged along, waiting for him to say what it was that he wanted to say.

Finally, he spoke. "They want my head," he said simply. "And I'm not going to give it to them without a fight. I'm not going to resign."

"Why do you think that?"

He snapped, "Because I know them. They've been waiting for something like his. Take my word for it. They want to settle old scores, real or imagined. First, they'll have their investigation. They'll find me lax in running the lab, in supervising O'Brien. They'll accuse me of putting undue pressure on Sanderson to be productive, of driving him to become a cheater. They'll even blame me for his disappearance.

Wait and see. I'm not paranoid about this. This is the way these things have ended up at other institutions when someone has to be sacrificed."

"But it wasn't your fault. It was Sanderson's. And anyway, you're a world-renowned figure. What would they gain from your disgrace? It would only harm the medical center and indirectly themselves."

Miller stopped at a divide in the trail and looked for a place to sit in the grass. Satisfied with a spot beneath an arch of trees, he unceremoniously dropped to the ground with his back against a tree trunk. Bergman sat in the grass next to him.

Plucking a long blade of grass from the ground, he picked at it methodically. "Paul, everything you're saying is true, but it won't stop them. This is too good an opportunity for them to humble me, to make me retire. They won't pass it up. But I'm not ready for the pasture yet. I've got work to do, programs to run, research to direct. I will *not* be put out to pasture."

"What can I do to help?"

Miller looked at Bergman with a spark of enthusiasm. "I have one long shot to pursue. I have to shift responsibility for this cheating business from my supposedly lax supervision to Sanderson himself. I have to show that Sanderson came to me as a cheater, that I didn't make him into one. I need someone to go back over his published medical-school research studies and talk with his preceptors. As loath as I am to say it, I have to find some dirt in his past. I'm going to ask you do this for me. I figure the dean's investigation will take two or three weeks, so that's how much time you'll have." He threw away what was left of the blade of grass and stared at Bergman with a pained smile on his face. "I know I'm asking a lot. At the least, it means hours going over articles as well as a trip to New Orleans for a few days to check up on his medical-school days. I know how devoted you are to Jennifer, but I have to ask anyway. For a variety of reasons, you're the one person I feel I can turn to in this matter."

Jennifer had said to be kind. "I'll do it," Bergman said softly. "Tell me how to do it and I'll do it."

Miller smiled gratefully, and they sat together on the grass going over the various strategies they would use to unlock the door to Sanderson's past.

CHAPTER

29

Bergman was in New Orleans a week after his conversation with Leo. As hot as the weather had been in the Northeast, he was totally unprepared for New Orleans. Even near the end of summer, the humidity was still unbearable. His hotel was on Royal Street in the French Quarter, and the smells of the area blended together in a—not very pleasant—pastiche. Because Miller had paid for his excursion out of his own pocket, he was on a tight budget. Nevertheless, the opportunity to visit a city he had never been to before, one with legendary eating establishments and the excitement of the Riverwalk with its view of the river replete with paddle-wheelers, was too much to ignore. Consequently, he crammed in as much touring as possible during his two-day stay.

It probably would have been even more pleasant had he been met with any enthusiasm at the medical school, but the opposite occurred. Although his visit to Dr. Nora Bennett had been arranged personally by Miller, it was obvious she was not happy to see him. Hostility oozed out of every pore of her well-lined face. She was the grand dame of Southern medicine and had been one of the longest reigning department chairpersons in the country. Dr. Bennett was less than pleased to learn that her pride and joy, Eric A Sanderson, III, had been accused of cheating and apparently hounded from his position. On Bergman's first visit to her small office at Charity Hospital, she wasted no time in setting the record straight.

"You Northerners have always treated us with contempt, and I suppose you always will. Whatever trouble Eric got himself into, I'm sure it was none of his doing. You all drove him to do it, on that I'll bet you whatever you want to wager."

"Ma'am," Bergman explained, "I'm a third-year fellow. I didn't drive Dr Sanderson to anything."

She shot him a disdainful look. "Why, of course, I didn't mean you personally. What kind of fool do you think I am? I meant your hospital and especially your boss, Leo Miller. He has a reputation for being an ornery creature, and I'm sure it's well deserved."

Sitting back in her chair, she surveyed her tiny quarters with an air of resignation. "Not much of a place to finish out your career, is it?" Her tone was softer now. "Twenty-three years as chief of medicine and 34 in the department over all, and this is how they put me out to pasture—a two-by-four closet in the oldest wing of the place. It's hard to believe, considering the suite I had at the medical school just a year ago. Still, I suppose I ought to be grateful I'm still active. I'm no spring chicken, you know." She stared straight at him. "How old do you think I am? Sixty? Sixty-five?"

Bergman nodded his head.

"What's that suppose to mean? Sixty or sixty-five?"

"Sixty," he said, figuring it never hurt to underestimate a woman's age. In reality, she looked about seventy. She had smoked too many cigarettes and drunk too many martinis, or gin fizzes, or whatever.

"Well, I'm seventy-four," she said delightedly. "How about that?"

He smiled meekly.

Pleased at having fooled him about her age, she now was ready to see exactly what it was he wanted from her.

"You enjoying New Orleans?" she asked.

"Yes."

"Not too hot for you? Don't lie."

"It's hot," he admitted.

"Hope you're good and uncomfortable. Serves you right for trying to impugn Eric Sanderson's character."

"That's not what I'm here for," he protested.

"That's what it sounds like to me. But get on with it and tell me what you want me to do."

He had already rehearsed his little speech with Miller, so he was able to deliver it with all the proper nuances. The plan was *not* to give Dr. Bennett the impression that her protégé had some kind of personality flaw.

"It's possible Dr. Sanderson's research habits have been characterized by cutting corners for some time," he began. "That's not to say that he was even consciously aware that he was doing something improper. It may just have been that in the rush to see his work published, he cut corners or did sloppy things that perhaps he shouldn't have. Now, while he was a house officer in your department, he published two papers, both of which were well-regarded when they appeared. In fact, they made enough of an impression on Dr. Miller that he accepted him into the fellowship without even interviewing him, which is quite unusual."

He stopped to catch his breath. Dr. Bennett sat quietly waiting for him to continue. "I brought reprints of the two papers with me," he said, "and I would appreciate it if you could answer a few questions about them."

"Fire away," she replied. The first paper was a report in a national cardiology journal, while the second was in a regional medical journal, the *Southern Journal of Medical Research*. The report in the cardiology journal concerned a series of Dr. Bennett's patients that Sanderson had followed for several years after they had been operated on for a form of congenital heart disease.

"He says he either saw these patients in your clinic or called them at their homes. Do you recall that?"

She thumbed through the papers without any apparent emotion. "Actually, I do recall it. There were ten patients and eight were examined at the hospital, as he stated. Very carefully, too, I might add. Now the other two were not up to the trip—they live out in the bayous—but he spoke with them extensively on the telephone. I know that too, because my office phone bill that month was monstrous as a result of those calls. I think that should satisfy you." Her smile was almost malicious in its delight. With studied detachment, she produced a pack of extra-long cigarettes from her purse and proceeded to light one with an old and well-tarnished lighter.

Bergman took out the second paper, which was actually the more interesting of the two. Sanderson had uncovered a family with an uncommon form of heart disease and had gone back into the family tree for five generations to show how the disease had been passed from father to son to daughter to son and so on.

"This was quite a bit of work," Dr. Bennett said between deep drags on the cigarette, as she thumbed through the reprint. "But it was worth it. It established for the first time that this condition could be passed down from generation to generation in this manner. When Eric presented this at the Southern Research Society meeting in Memphis that year, it made him almost a celebrity." She smiled sadly and shook her head from side to side. "And now look at him. Disgraced, maybe dead. Whoever would have thought it? Did he deserve such an end? I ask you in all honesty, did he?" She threw the Xerox copy back in Bergman's lap. For a moment, he thought she was going to cry. Then she reached back and retrieved it. He thought turning the pages for her was like turning back the years. She put the cigarette down and read aloud from the discussion section. There was no question that Sanderson had written his papers with clarity and force.

"You know," she went on, "when this was first presented it was something of a sensation, because it was the first such report. But within a year, another family like this was reported in Wisconsin, and then a few months ago, I read another one was documented in California. So his observations have been amply confirmed—which is only fitting. Look at the work that went into this." She turned the paper towards him so that he could see the five-generation family tree that Sanderson had displayed in a huge figure that stretched over the entire length of the page. "He spent nights going over the family records to verify the dates of the marriages, the birth of the children, everything."

There were over a hundred family members listed, going back over 150 years. Bergman wondered how he could have gotten enough records to verify the data, yet everything seemed to fit neatly into place. But wasn't that his trademark? Making everything fit into place? When he had first looked over the two papers in Miller's office—with Miller looking over his shoulder as well—he had seen nothing out of order, nor had Miller. Now something about that family tree puzzled him, but he couldn't put his finger on it.

"A tremendous accomplishment," Dr. Bennett concluded, "and one that we're all proud of. I can still see Eric presenting that data at the Southern Society meeting, his blond hair shining in the spotlight on the speaker's podium; he was as poised and confident as could be, Dr. Bergman. Now you people maligned him and disgraced him." She said it coldly but impersonally, as if the "you" did not refer specifically to him. But, of course, if she had known all the facts, she surely would have regarded Bergman as one of the instruments in Sanderson's fall from grace.

"I suppose you'd like to go out to the country courthouse and recheck his data. It's not far from here, and I'm sure you'll spend a busy day or two at it. But no air-conditioning, I'm afraid," she said with a smirk.

The thought was not a pleasant one. He wondered how far Miller expected him to carry out this investigation. "I don't think that will be necessary," he said, and her face lit up.

"Well, that's the first encouraging thing I've heard you say. You must trust me after all," she said with a smile.

"It's not you we doubted, Dr. Bennett."

"Don't give me that crap. If you weren't questioning my supervisory capabilities, you wouldn't have made the trip. Leo Miller sent you here on a fishing expedition. You know it, and I know it. But the fish aren't jumping today." She laughed.

His acknowledgment that he would not be going into the courthouse files seemed to relax her considerably. Her tone grew almost warm.

"Now, I have a pleasant surprise for you." She leaned over and lowered her voice to an almost conspiratorial whisper. "I shouldn't be doing this, but you seem like a nice young man whose boss put him in an awkward position. Can you guess who just happens to be an in-patient here at the Charity Hospital at this very minute?"

He had no idea.

"The very latest member of the Garrett family, the one that Eric wrote up, the first family with the strange familial cardiac disorders. Want to see him?"

He really didn't. He felt like a beaten man, and all he wanted to do was get on a plane and go home. But her look was so entreating, he reluctantly agreed. He figured he owed her a few minutes for putting up with him in the first place.

Dr. Bennett led him downstairs into the patient areas. These were still made up of six- and eight-bed wards, a throwback to the old days of hospital medicine in the United States, and that's where he encountered Hiram Garrett. He was a pleasant enough middle-aged man, slightly short of breath even in bed. Dr. Bennett chatted amiably with him for several minutes, then introduced Bergman. "Dr. Bergman's from up north. He's interested in Dr. Eric Sanderson's research into your family. You remember Dr. Sanderson, don't you?"

"Deed I do," Garrett replied. "He spent a lot of time with me and my sisters tracing the family tree and finding out who had heart disease and who didn't."

Bergman had brought the research paper with him, and he looked again at the diagram of the family tree. "I'm amazed he was able to trace your relative back for so many generations. He was obviously a hard worker."

"Yup, he would question us for hours at a time."

Bergman referred again to the family tree. "I suppose he spent hours at the county courthouse checking into the earliest records of your ancestry as well."

"Well, I don't know about that. We didn't talk much about the real early relatives."

"Oh, I remember that he did," Dr. Bennett added, as much for Bergman's edification as the patient's. "In fact, he made a point of having me drop him off at the courthouse and pick him up several hours later. Did that a few times. I must say it was a nuisance."

Garrett looked at her peculiarly, but said nothing.

Something tickled Bergman's curiosity. "You look puzzled, Mr. Garrett."

Garrett stared at him, the stranger from the north, and then at Dr. Bennett, the stern symbol of southern matriarchal authority, and continued to maintain his silence.

"Yes, I remember those afternoons at the Jefferson Parish Courthouse as if it were yesterday," Dr. Bennett added as an afterthought. From what she told colleagues later, who subsequently told Bergman, she always regretted that addendum.

Now Garrett really looked perturbed. His breathing quickened.

"You alright, Mr. Garrett?" Bergman ventured, solicitously.

Maybe it was Bergman's concern that got to him; maybe it was his own conscience.

"We're not from Jefferson Parish," Garrett said quietly.

"What's that?" Dr. Bennett asked.

"Our family's not from Jefferson Parish," the patient responded.

"Where are you from?" Bergman asked.

"St. Bernard Parish."

"I don't understand," Dr. Bennett went on. "Why would Dr. Sanderson spend so much time going over records at the Jefferson Parish Courthouse?"

"Can't say, Ma'am."

Dr. Bennett looked at Bergman. "This is ridiculous. He must be confused. If the Garrett's were from St. Bernard Parish, Eric would have gone over the records there."

Bergman looked at the article. Jefferson Parish was clearly listed as the family seat, yet here was Garrett saying it wasn't so. Bergman was confused as well, but Garrett cleared up the mystery.

"He couldn't have checked records at the St. Bernard Parish Courthouse. It burned down in 1968. All the old records were destroyed."

Dr. Bennett sighed. Bergman shook his head in wonder. Sanderson had done it again— cut corners when he didn't have to. There was enough data on enough family members to make a convincing case, but no, he had to show the disease had been spread from 1765 onward, instead of being content with just the last three generations. He pretended to be looking up records, while probably writing his next paper.

"You think he cheated, don't you?" Her tone was markedly subdued.

"Not only am I thinking it, but I'm saying it out loud. And I'm delighted to say it. Not because it will cause you embarrassment, but because it will exonerate Leo Miller as being responsible for corrupting Sanderson's character, or by coddling him and encouraging him to cut corners. So excuse me for being terribly excited—and happy, yes happy! I can't help myself for feeling that way." He smiled broadly, not caring if she was offended.

"I don't want to know how happy you are!" she shouted at him. "Get the hell out of New Orleans." Her look of disgust followed him out the door.

CHAPTER

30

On the flight back from New Orleans, Bergman reflected on what he had learned and how it might help Leo Miller in the upcoming investigation. The more he thought about it, the more he realized that the revelations about Sanderson's past life were no guarantee that Leo would be exonerated of any wrong doing. It all depended on the attitude of the "judge and jury." They could either use this information for Leo's benefit or they could downplay its significance if they saw fit. But who would be involved in that pseudo-judicial process? That Bergman didn't know.

When he told Jennifer about his experiences, she wasn't very surprised.

"Not one of my favorite people. He does what he has to do to get ahead," she observed.

"A story as old as time itself."

"Maybe I'm too naïve, but I've never known anyone like that."

Jennifer laughed that easy, tinkling laugh that he had come to love. "You are naïve. You're in the wrong profession. All a psychotherapist does all day long is to listen to confessions like that. Amongst others."

"More confessions than a priest?"

However surprised he was and however unperturbed Jennifer was, Miller's reaction was as expected. The next morning in his office, when Bergman told him what he had discovered in New Orleans, Miller was elated.

"A lucky hunch pays off, thanks to you, Paul. I must admit I was afraid at first I was just sending you on a useless fishing expedition, a waste of time. But as it turns out, I think we've hit the lottery. I can't see Harrison wanting to pursue this once I let him know about Sanderson's past."

"You think they'll call the whole investigation off?"

"No, of course not; they can't do that. But they'll have an easy way out."

"If they want one."

He nodded grimly. "Yes you're right. If they want one."

It was on that ambiguous note that they parted. The academic year had come to an end several weeks ago, and the hospital's senior residents and subspecialty fellows had departed. A new crop had entered for the annual July 1st ritual. Bergman immersed himself in the orientation of the new fellows. This year, however, he occupied a more exalted position since he was not only a third-year fellow, but was also a junior member of the faculty—Instructor of Medicine. Miller had arranged the faculty appointment in consideration of his increased teaching role with both the medical students and the house staff. The early days of the new academic year passed quickly. Between his teaching assignments and research endeavors, he had little time for other pursuits, and what time he did have, he spent with Jennifer. Signs of her pregnancy were now obvious, and they hoped the summer months would not prove too uncomfortable for her. Since the baby was not expected until early October, the most uncomfortable times would occur when the summer's heat was past.

Nothing more was said to him by Miller about the hospital's investigation into the Sanderson affair, and Bergman assumed that it had been defused by his detective work in New Orleans. Around this time, Miller's retraction notices started to appear in those journals that had published Sanderson's earlier papers from Miller's lab. Although Miller had notified the NIH administrators several months ago of the problem with Sanderson's work, he had heard nothing from them. Now, however, notice of the retraction seemed to arouse them from their inattentiveness. Within a week, an NIH investigative team—one physician and one staff person—visited the lab to take preliminary notes. They poured over all the documents that had been assembled and sent to the dean's office. Their arrival jolted the hospital's own investigation back to life and, much to Miller's dismay, what had seemed like a dwindling spark was now fanned anew into a bright flame.

When Bergman had the opportunity to spend a few moments alone with him in late July, Miller told him what he feared most.

"The Federal government is obsessed with cheating on NIH grants. There's a congressional oversight committee chaired by a representative from California, Winchell, I think his name is, that's made a name for itself and its chairman by uncovering all sorts of mud and slime in the hallowed halls of medical academia. Unfortunately, I've heard from a friend in the dean's office that the committee is really going to sink its teeth into my hide."

"But why you? You haven't done anything wrong. I mean, it was Sanderson who did the cheating, not you." Miller shook his head gloomily. "Sanderson's a small fry. The Congressman really likes to catch bigger fish, those who try to whitewash these things. Remember what he did to that Nobel Laureate in New York who tried to defend one of his lab workers who falsified animal research on cancer?"

"Vaguely"

"Well, it's a good lesson for us all. That's what these congressional committees love. Winchell even got the Secret Service involved to show the New York data slips were forged! And the month before, his committee embarrassed the hell out of one of the California schools for misappropriating federal grant funds to do over their university president's office. I mean they love this stuff."

"Alright, so assume the worse. It's embarrassing, that's all."

Miller shook his head again. "Yes, in some places it would just be embarrassing. But here, I get the distinct impression that it could get me fired."

Bergman tried to reassure him, but his heart wasn't in it. He had a feeling Miller was right. The next day, as if on cue, one of the investigators from the NIH arranged to meet with Bergman. He was accompanied by a staff member from Congressman Winchell's committee.

"We're just gathering data at this point," the NIH representative explained. "We have to do it anytime the terms of one of our grants are violated." He was a thin, red-headed young man with a boyish face and an absolutely unthreatening manner. His companion, on the other hand, was a hatched-face swarthy type who said little, constantly wrote on a pad, and scared the hell out of Bergman.

Bergman explained patiently to both of them that Sanderson appeared to have had a basic personality disorder that led him to cheat to achieve his goals. He cited the work Sanderson had done in New Orleans which, incidentally, he had learned only that morning that Dr. Bennett had asked to be retracted from the journal that had published it. But the hardest part was explaining what took Leo so long in accusing Sanderson.

"It sounds like he was trying to protect him," the blond questioner concluded. "Not an unnatural reaction by any means."

"Presumed innocent until proven guilty," Bergman reminded him.

"Or, obtaining time to prepare a cover-up?" The red-headed young man no longer appeared benign. "Perhaps a little bit of both," the hatched-faced representative said almost kindly, reminding Bergman not to judge character by appearance.

"Once it was clear what happened, Dr. Miller acted promptly and thoroughly," Bergman said, with all the conviction he could muster.

The young NIH man shrugged. "One could argue that the delay further destabilized Sanderson and led to his emotional collapse. Perhaps more decisiveness earlier on would have been better for all concerned."

Bergman couldn't argue with that. It was a reasonable point. The federal team stayed another day to conduct more interviews. Word spread quickly about their presence, and the town newspaper picked up the story with zeal. Jennifer commented on the developments that night over dinner.

"I smell more wolves circling for the kill. Your boss is certainly a juicy target."

"There's nothing to it," Bergman insisted. "Just publicity for some congressman."

"Yes, but what effect will that have on the medical-school administration?"

She put down her fork. "Why should they continue to be embarrassed because of him? Wouldn't it be better to serve him up as a sacrificial lamb?"

"Leo the lion becomes Leo the lamb," Bergman mused softly.

Jennifer nodded and resumed her meal. "Oh, by the way, I forgot to tell you about this weird postcard I got in the mail. Here, let me show you."

After rummaging through some papers on her desk, she produced the card. It was addressed to her and consisted of only one sentence: "One if by land, two if by sea ... and baby makes three." There was no signature, just a question-mark.

"Crazy, huh?"

"The postmark is local. Must be a riddle from one of our friends."

"You think?"

"Sure," he said reassuringly. "What else could it be?"

CHAPTER

31

Several days after they had left, the two-man team from Washington returned to the campus, now joined by a young female physician whose questions were even sharper than those of her blond companion. Everyone who was interviewed found the experience to be a distinctly unpleasant one, not so much because of the questions that were asked, but *how* they were asked. This was clearly not a truth-seeking venture; this was a vendetta against someone already judged to be guilty. All this, despite the fact that they had never even met Leo Miller (and probably never heard about him) before the Sanderson affair took place!

As far as the Congressional committee was concerned, or so it seemed, this was as good a case as any to make another example of the arrogance of "elite" universities in squandering tax-payers' funds earmarked for research. Congressman Winchell had made this his personal crusade and, indeed, he had uncovered some deplorable instances of both abuse of federal funding and shady research processes. But as one of the other fellows commented to Bergman, politicians who were interested in worthy causes still were politicians. Since the primary aim of a successful politician is to be re-elected, and since this is an every-two-year ordeal for Congressmen, a constant supply of media headlines is essential. No matter how weak the facts, the case against Leo Miller would supply still more grist for the publicity mill, at least for the short term. Bergman thought his colleague's evaluation of politicians a bit harsh, but since the new fellow was from Chicago, Bergman knew how his suspicions might have been nurtured.

All during the investigation, from the time Douglas had done the initial whistle-blowing to the arrival of the visitors from Washington, the day-to-day life of the medical center had proceeded at its usual frantic pace. Miller still found time to conduct his weekly Chief's Rounds, to care for individual patients referred to him, and to oversee the running of the division and its research efforts. But, in the last several weeks, Bergman thought he detected the beginning of a wearing-down trend. Miller's gait lost some of its spring; his words were often inaudible to the collection of house officers, fellows, and nurses who trailed him on rounds.

Fortunately, Miller could arouse himself when the occasion demanded it. When the wife of the university president was admitted to the CCU with what appeared to be a heart attack, he made himself instantly available. It turned out to be no more than a panic attack, but instead of casually dismissing her complaints as soon as heart disease was ruled out by the tests—as most of his colleagues and fellows did—he spent several hours at her bedside, calming and reassuring her, and generally making her feel that she was *not* a hypochondriac, that her complaints were real, and that because they were based on functional rather than organic problems, they should respond to appropriate psychotherapy and, perhaps, medications. It was a *tour de force* and impressed all who witnessed it, not the least the woman's husband, who pledged eternal gratitude.

"Did all this tender loving care have some subliminal political considerations?" Bergman asked him mischievously when the woman was finally discharged. Bergman supposed it was a sign of their increasingly close relationship that he would even offer such a suggestion.

"If it did, it wouldn't do me any good, anyway. The President is a no-nonsense kind of guy who'd fire his own mother if he thought it necessary. No, I expect no "secondary compensation" from my good deeds. I did it for the old-fashioned reasons—good patient care and compassion." He said it unemotionally, which meant Bergman hadn't offended him at all.

A week later, though, Bergman was able to see him in a highly emotional state over a patient's well-being, and it was a good experience, not just for Bergman, but for all those at the medical center who liked and respected their Chief of Cardiology. The patient this time was no one important in the university community—nor was it someone referred from someone who was rich and famous—but, still, the circumstances brought out the best in Leo Miller and helped recharge those depleted batteries that energized his failing *joie de vivre*.

The patient, who suffered a massive heart attack, was not unknown to the medical school—quite the contrary. Hector Garcia was one of the "garbagemen," responsible for the daily collection of green and brown trash bags that collected in the offices, labs, halls, etc. Contents of the waste-paper baskets and similar receptacles would be emptied into these bags by a clean-up crew in the early morning hours and then Hector would appear and make sure they were gathered and brought down to the collection area in the basement for loading onto a truck bound for a nearby incinerator. Sometimes he had the aid of a cart, sometimes he didn't. Sometimes the service elevator worked, sometimes it didn't. Before his hospitalization, it didn't matter to Hector. If he had to carry the bags on his back, he would. Miller learned about his extra efforts and his treks on the stairs. He pressured the hospital for a raise for Hector, which the poor man could really use. Thanks to Miller, he got it.

When Hector was done with Miller's lab and offices, he went to other floors. He was usually finished by three a.m., but if he had to stay longer, he did. Because overtime requests were discouraged by the economy-minded hospital administrators (except for nursing or technical staff), he rarely requested extra compensation. What was behind Hector's good-hearted approach? Gratitude, plain and simple. A Nicaraguan, he had been caught up in the struggle between Sandinistas and Contras. (His village was in no-man's land.) After having seen one of his young children killed in crossfire, he packed up his wife and two other children and somehow managed to immigrate to the US. He received sanctuary in several churches and finally, two years earlier, had been granted political asylum. To have a job with good wages in a country where political freedom was accepted without a second thought was as close to heaven as he could imagine. He spoke only Pidgin English, but his face always communicated the message he wanted: thank you, friends, one and all.

Hector's only bad habit was cigarette smoking. He was almost, but not quite, a chain smoker. Whether that was the main ingredient in his heart disease was questionable. The carrying of the heavy bags certainly didn't help the situation.

Whatever the precipitating factors, at a little after eight p.m., on a warm but not oppressive night in early August, Hector Garcia came to the emergency room with all the classic signs of a massive heart attack: chest pains, extensive shortness of breath, and cool, clammy skin—a tell-tale sign of a rapidly failing circulation. His complexion was ashen and in his eyes was the wild look of someone who couldn't catch his breath and knew he was dying.

Bergman was on call that night and when he got to the ER Hector's face beseeched him for help. His words were garbled; Bergman couldn't make them out but he knew what he was trying to say: "Save me." The ER team had inserted an intravenous line in his left arm and peppered his chest with ECG leads. The signal on their machine did not look good. There were runs of markedly irregular beats and his blood pressure was barely palpable. After the ER team sat him up, Bergman was able to listen to his lungs with his stethoscope; fluid was filling both sides. It would only be a matter of minutes before it came bubbling out of his mouth. He would drown in his own body water.

"Intubate him now!" he ordered the ER team. "Stat!" An anesthesiologist working in one of the side rooms on an accident victim was notified and sent his colleague running over to Hector's cubicle. Hector Garcia was too weak to fight the breathing tube, and it was quickly inserted. A few minutes later he became unconscious, and Bergman feared they were going to lose him.

"Start the pressors," he told the nurse, and the heart stimulants began to flow into Hector's intravenous line from the plastic bags suspended on metal poles by his stretcher. While the drugs poured into his system, respiratory therapists hooked up the breathing tube to a mechanical ventilator, supplying oxygen under pressure to his damaged lungs. Slowly Hector's blood pressure returned to near-normal levels; his eyes opened and he seemed to understand that the ER team was fighting to save him. They began an infusion of a clot-busting drug and prepared to move him upstairs to the CCU.

The rest of the night was touch and go. Bergman called Miller to let him know that one of his "people" was in trouble and, to his surprise, he joined Bergman in the CCU near midnight.

"I can't believe he came through all the hell in Nicaragua to die in our hospital of a lousy heart attack," Miller said, after Bergman had presented the case to him.

"It doesn't look good," Bergman responded gloomily. Even after it seemed the blocked coronary artery had opened, his condition continued to deteriorate.

"We'll pull out all the stops," Miller decided. "I don't care if it is the middle of the night. Alert the cath team for an emergency intra-aortic balloon insertion followed by coronary angioplasty. We'll open up every blockage we can find. If that doesn't save him, nothing will. The cardiac surgeons probably won't touch him with a ten-foot pole at this stage, so it's up to us."

Donovan, the cath-lab director, arrived 20 minutes later, and the rest of the team soon followed. Using the expertise developed with years of training, they quickly inserted a long tube through one of Garcia's thigh arteries. This special catheter was attached to a pump that regularly inflated and deflated a balloon. When positioned in the body's main blood vessel, the aorta, the balloon was able to augment the heart's pumping ability, now reduced markedly by the massive heart attack. From the other thigh, another set of catheters was inserted to the point where the aorta spun off the blood vessels that supplied the heart muscle itself. Injections of dye—which could be followed on video screens in the catheterization laboratory—told the team where the blockages were located. Delving into their bag of tricks, Donovan and his colleagues threaded another type of special catheter through the narrowed opening of the coronary arteries and then inflated a smaller balloon. This device resembled the one placed in the aorta to assist the heart, but because it was in a narrower space and under high pressure, the smaller balloon could "press" the fatty blockage against the vessel wall and create a larger opening.

While all this was going on, Miller had donned a face mask and protective lead gown (to shield him from X-rays) and joined the team in the specially-designed procedure room. He followed every development closely, occasionally offering words of encouragement to Garcia, who remained semi-alert during the procedure. When everything seemed to be going well, Miller stepped out of the procedure room and rejoined the small group that had been watching the scene through a large window in the wall: Bergman, Goldberg (the CCU director), and several of the fellows. It was almost three a.m.

"Donovan did a great job. I think Hector's going to make it," Miller said, as he removed his mask. "Ten years ago he would have been a goner for sure, but not today." He smiled broadly. "You'll think I'm nuts, guys, but it's a wonderful feeling to be able to see the advances we've made in saving people's lives. Makes me feel good I chose this profession." He stripped off the lead gown and hung it up. The catheterization team was finishing up with Garcia, getting ready to transport him to the CCU, where Goldberg and his team would take over his care. The transport itself was a cumbersome procedure, since the patient was not only attached to a respirator unit, but also the pump part of the intra-aortic balloon device. Walking slowly, the team of doctors and nurses navigated the hallway between the catheterization laboratory and the CCU while pushing the patient's bed, also maneuvering the various pieces of equipment to which he was attached.

Once Garcia was safely ensconced in a room, Miller went to the visitor's area and met with Hector's wife. Bergman accompanied him. He reassured her that her husband was going to "make it," but he avoided giving any hard and fast long-term prediction. Mrs. Garcia was appreciative, nevertheless. Upon returning to the catheterization laboratory area to congratulate Donovan's team on a job well done, Bergman was surprised to hear one of the new fellows complaining about the long hours he was putting in. "I'm up half of the night for some garbageman. By the attention he's getting, you'd think he was the President of the United States."

Bergman could imagine the hair on Miller's neck bristling when he heard that comment. And, indeed, Miller wheeled suddenly and approached his newest trainee, an obviously worn-out young Kansan named Jones.

"We treat *all* of our patients the same, doctor," Miller said firmly, "no matter what their job, or their background, or their ability to pay.

As far as I'm concerned, that garbageman is the President of the United States. Do you understand me?"

Dr. Jones shriveled in his chair. Miller repeated his question. "Do you understand me?"

The trainee nodded meekly.

Miller turned to Bergman. "We're not training these young people properly. Maybe it's my fault; maybe I've been too distant lately, too preoccupied with my own problems. I can't let those bastards make me forget I'm still a doctor. Hector Garcia taught me that all over again." Miller reached for his white coat. "It's funny, Paul, but tonight has been like a breath of fresh air. I feel like myself again." He put on his coat and walked back toward his office. Despite the hour, there was no question he had a new spring in his step. Leo Miller was definitely girding his loins for the battle to come.

CHAPTER

32

Garcia's recovery was slow, but steady. The entire cardiology section followed his progress avidly. Most of them had participated in his care in one way or another, and it was a mark of pride in their work that this man had been snatched from death's door. A steady stream of visitors helped to keep his spirits up, as first he was weaned from the respirator, and then the balloon pump, and finally the pressor agents that helped support his circulation. The visitors cut across all of the usual political groups in his native Nicaragua. Garcia was truly a man without enemies.

Bergman wished the same could have been said about Leo Miller. He seemed to be accumulating enemies. Just when it appeared a lull had been reached and, perhaps, the tide of misfortune was ebbing away, Congressman Winchell's female investigator returned to the campus. Perhaps because of his gangster-like appearance, Bergman had been initially wary of the swarthy, hatchet-faced investigator and given short shrift to the other two, first the red-headed young man but especially the attractive brunette who was the last initially to arrive on the scene. That turned out to have been a mistake as well. Ms. Stuart was sharp as a tack and extremely persistent. Her visit during the last week of August was ominous from the beginning. Through the hospital employees' grapevine, Miller learned from one of his technicians that Winchell's aide was delving into matters far removed from the Sanderson affair.

Miller stopped Bergman in the hall one morning. "She's going around interviewing Asian students about their reaction to Miller's turning down the Chrysanthemum Medal. What in the world does that have to do with anything?"

Bergman told him he hadn't the foggiest idea. Later that week, they heard she had moved on from the Asian students to the African-Americans. What was she up to, Bergman wondered.

On the last day of August she interviewed Miller again, and he asked Bergman to sit in on the meeting and take notes.

"Is this really necessary?" Ms. Stuart said, apparently not amused by Bergman's presence.

"I think so," Miller replied firmly. His intuition had told him to expect the worst, and it seemed he was right on the money.

Ms. Stuart got right to the point. "Dr. Miller, the more we learn about you, the more our committee is concerned by your apparent negative attitude towards our investigation."

"It does have some elements of a witch-hunt, doesn't it?"

"Not as far as we are concerned. Your conduct in this cheating episode is being investigated by your own university, the NIH, and by a congressional-oversight committee. You do admit there was academic cheating in a federally funded grant, don't you?"

"I haven't denied it."

"Then all the inquiries are appropriate."

"Are they? The young man in question is missing. If he were still here, his career as a researcher would be over—as it should be. But why this vendetta to punish the rest of us? His immediate supervisor in the laboratory has acknowledged improper supervision, and his career is probably ruined as well. And my own name has been besmudged, far out of proportion to my role in this whole matter."

"You were very slow to reveal the fraud; some would even say you covered it up."

"Baloney! I investigated it, found it to have occurred, and was about to take remedial action when Dr. Sanderson disappeared."

"There are many people on this case who believe you acted slowly because the fellow who first came to you with evidence was an African-American and not trustworthy."

Bergman thought Miller was going to hit her. Bergman put a restraining hand on his arm, but he angrily brushed it aside.

"That's too ridiculous to even dignify with an answer."

"Isn't it also true that you think so little of the Asian students that you refused one of the biggest awards the Japanese can bestow on a foreigner?"

Now his mouth gaped in astonishment. Bergman also couldn't believe what he was hearing.

Miller laughed. "This is political correctness gone crazy. This hogwash of yours won't go very far with the university authorities."

Ms. Stuart shrugged. "We'll see."

Miller and Bergman exchanged looks of incredulity.

The next day the town tabloid splashed the Congressman's allegation across its front page, attributing it only to its own investigators, but clearly someone from the Congressman's office had "leaked" the information. The desired effect occurred. When the dean returned the next week, he immediately re-convened his own ad-hoc investigative committee.

CHAPTER

33

Summer in the western half of Massachusetts comes to an end even before August does. The nights turn surprisingly cool in just a few days' time. If the natives are lucky, there will be a true Indian summer in late September, but, for all intents and purposes, by the last week in August it's already time to dig out the autumn sweaters. Labor Day fell on September 1st that year and, in some parts of the county, frost was reported.

For the newlyweds, it had been a relatively quiet time compared to the hurly-burly of the spring, but there was a good side as well. Jennifer had been very uncomfortable during the summer heat; now, the cooler air lessened the strain of the enlarging basketball that her waist had become. The other troublesome aspect of the summer had been the postcards: the first had been followed by another, two weeks later, and every two weeks since. The message was the always the same. "Who do you think is sending these cards?" Jennifer said with exasperation.

Bergman shrugged. "I don't know."

"Should we be concerned? I mean, there is something menacing about them."

"Is there? I don't think so."

"I need a hug."

He obliged and went off to work smiling, but with a nagging thought on his mind that the postcards were more than a prank.

At the hospital, Bergman was supposed to be planning the list of speakers to invite for the monthly lecture series that ran from October to May, but he was distracted by the newspapers lying on the floor beside his desk. The tabloid continued to feature the Congressional committee's outrage in its pages. The broadside was less seedy, but now it, too, had picked up the scent. A less spectacular and more thoughtful story was featured in that day's edition.

The reporter did not have the same access to Ms. Stuart as the tabloid's investigative reporter apparently did. Consequently, the issues raised by the tabloid were examined by the rival newspaper with some skepticism, especially those concerning complaints by various minority groups. Nonetheless, the combined result of both articles was an upsurge of interest in the Sanderson affair. There were also those conspiracy theorists who were still arguing that Sanderson's disappearance really had been a cover-up for one or another aspect of the cheating scandals.

As a result of the publicity, the corridors of the hospital were abuzz with whispered conversations about the newspaper stories for several days. Only when Miller himself strode into sight would the buzzing suddenly cease. Once he left, the conversation resumed. Occasionally, the cardiology staffers were corralled into a corner and asked to render an opinion. "Say, what if . . . ?" Or "Is it true that . . . ?" Not uncommonly, they also were confronted with "I heard Miller's going to resign. Right, or wrong?" Most of them just shrugged and continued walking on. They had no more information than the questioners and, even if they had, they wouldn't have shared it.

Miller himself was clearly expecting the other shoe to hit the floor once the details of the Congressional committee's outcome were in the newspapers. "What can I do?" he asked Bergman on the way to lunch. "Wait for them to decide what *they're* going to do and then react to it. The ball's not in my court, not that it ever really was."

In the crowded cafeteria they found a quiet table at the back, near the huge picture window that looked out over rolling farmlands. "The leaves will start turning early this year," Leo said. "Once Labor Day comes, it's my time of the year all over again."

"A good omen," Bergman offered between bites of a sandwich.

Miller laughed. "Oh, for the brashness of youth. If you still believe in omens, Dr. Paul Bergman, then you probably also believe in Santa Claus and pigs that fly. No, my young friend, omens aren't for me."

Donovan saw them and pulled up a chair. As usual, he was in a rush. Lunch had to be crammed in between two emergency coronary arteriograms. "How's your patient Garcia doing, Leo? Back to work yet?" Miller smiled. "Hector is progressing, but I told him—and his supervisor—he has to lay off the heavy-duty work for a long time. They're trying to find something lighter for him to do. But most importantly, I got him to stop smoking. Or at least, I think I did." He laughed easily.

"Heard anything from the dean yet?"

"No," Miller replied, "nothing yet, but I was just telling Paul that I'm sure I will."

Donovan consumed his sandwich in a matter of minutes, then got up to leave. "Back to the cath lab. Let me know if I can be of any help when the call does come."

"Thank you. I'll remember that."

After he left, Miller turned to Bergman and smiled again. "What a great staff. They've all said what Donovan said: "I'm there if and when you need me." It's a good feeling, believe me."

"That goes for me, too, of course."

"I know it does, Paul, and I appreciate it."

Lunch over; they walked back to Miller's office to go over an article Bergman wanted to submit to the *American Cardiology Journal*.

Miller's secretary seemed relieved to see him. "I've been looking all over for you, Dr. Miller. I was just going to have the page operator start buzzing you."

"What's the problem?"

"The dean and department chairman are on their way over. They said it was important."

Miller stayed calm. "Come on in, Paul. You can be a witness to my fortitude during the Tom and Jerry Cartoon Show. Or maybe, Abbott and Costello are more appropriate." Over Bergman's protests, he made him sit in a chair on one side of the room while he awaited his visitors. Bergman didn't want to be there, but what could he do? If Miller needed his presence, if it was important to him, then he would stay. Busying himself with some papers on his desk, Miller barely looked up when his secretary ushered in Jack Smiley and Harrison Wentworth. After a moment, he put away the papers and said, "Good afternoon, gentlemen," with a thin smile on his lips. "Make yourselves comfortable. Oh, and don't worry about Dr. Bergman, I've asked him to stay."

Harrison shrugged. "As you wish." The dean said nothing.

An uneasy silence prevailed. Miller stared at his two antagonists, and they stared right back.

The dean began. "This is not a pleasant task, Leo. Not for me, nor for Harrison, and certainly not for you, but I'm afraid we have little choice in the matter. Isn't that right, Harrison?" The department chairman nodded silently.

"When I returned from my vacation and learned that Congressman Winchell's committee had visited our medical center for yet another visit, I was concerned. This concern turned to anger when I learned that, in addition to the scientific cheating scandal, the Federal investigators were now looking into charges of minority discrimination of one type or another."

"All totally bullshit," Miller interrupted angrily.

"Be that as it may, certainly at face value the whole affair seems very damaging to your credibility and, of course, to the medical school's reputation."

"I think I've acted appropriately in this matter," Miller replied more calmly. "You can question the timing of some of my actions, but, on the whole, my actions were well-intentioned. No cover-up was attempted, and full responsibility was accepted by me and Dr. O'Brien for what, in retrospect, turns out to be the results of a sick mind at work in our animal laboratory."

Now it was the dean's turn to get angry. "That's your opinion, Leo. We take a different view, and apparently, so do a lot of other concerned observers. My investigative committee, in particular, as well as Congressman Winchell. Under the circumstances, I think it would be best if you resign as Chief of Cardiology."

Miller showed no emotion. "Is this your wish as well, Harrison?"

"It is," the department chairman replied, with unusual firmness.

The possibility of Miller's resignation had, of course, been a topic of conversation among both his friends and enemies since the Sanderson affair unraveled, so it was not really a surprise to Miller or Bergman to hear the dean actually say the words. Bergman was on the edge of his seat waiting to hear Miller's response. Based on Miller's rejuvenation since Garcia's illness, Bergman had no doubt he was prepared to fight it.

"I will not resign," Miller said.

Wentworth sighed. "In that case . . ."

"I'll handle this," the dean interrupted. "In that case, you will be removed administratively. Dr. Wentworth will appoint someone to replace you until a search can be made for a new chief. You should be prepared to surrender your office and secretary to your replacement as soon as possible. Other adjustments may be necessary as well. And you may consider it wise to seek another position elsewhere."

Bergman was surprised. He had never contemplated this degree of maliciousness. Miller seemed calm, dispassionate.

"I challenge your right to do this," Miller said. "I have not been accorded due process, and I feel I have the right to such process."

"I can remove division chiefs whenever I want to," Harrison said.

"Only for due cause," Miller insisted.

"Debatable—no one ever fights this and wins."

"I will," Miller said evenly. "I am going to go to the President of the University and demand that this matter be referred to a neutral panel for adjudication. I want this matter discussed fully and fairly, and I want my own observer at the meetings to assure fairness. I have good reason to believe that the President will grant these requests."

Wentworth was stunned. It was clear he had never contemplated such an outcome. His mouth fell open, and he turned to the dean in obvious puzzlement. "Can he do this?"

Smiley remained poker-faced. "He can try. But even if he succeeds, he'll gain nothing because people on that panel will make sure our case is heard. Either that, or I'll resign." He locked eyes with Miller. "You'll probably get your panel, Leo, but there's no way in hell they will undo what's been done. Come on, Harrison, I think we've ended our visit."

Barely 15 minutes had transpired between their arrival and departure, but it seemed like hours, so heavy had the air become. Miller rose from his desk and began pacing the room. "I anticipated this little scene and visited the President and his wife two nights ago. Delightful woman, his wife. I'm sure you remember her during her stay in the

CCU." He looked at Bergman with a twinkle in his eyes. "Yes, I know I told you then that there was no way to influence the President, but I also told you he was a fair man. That's all I asked for from him—fairness. Whatever his panel recommends, I will do. I'm not going to pursue this to the courts—that I reassured him. This panel's meetings should make for some lively sessions, at the least. I'm sure you'll find them interesting."

"Me?" Bergman said, puzzled. "Why me?"

"Yes you, Paul. You're going to be my observer."

"But . . ."

"Please don't argue. I need you to do this—you will do it, won't you?" His hawk-like eyes bore into Bergman, who knew he couldn't refuse his mentor.

"Of course," Bergman answered, "I would be pleased to."

"Good", Miller said smiling. "And don't worry, I'll win."

Of that, Bergman wasn't so sure.

CHAPTER

34

The wording of the University President's announcement was a tribute to his experience as a former diplomat (US Ambassador to Morocco for three years). Nothing was said about countermanding the dean's order relieving Miller of his chiefship. That would have raised unnecessary ruffles in the bureaucratic hierarchy that ran the medical school and hospital. No, removing a section chief was clearly a prerogative of the pertinent department head as well as the dean. What the President was doing was simply summoning a broad-based panel to examine the issue of academic cheating on campus and "related" issues. If the panel were to recommend that the dean reevaluate Miller's dismissal, so be it; if not, that would end the challenge. That's all the President could do, he told Miller and, in reality, that is more than Miller was entitled to; section chiefs served at the pleasure of their department chairman. Of course, their status as tenured professors did safeguard other financial and academic aspects of their position.

By anticipating what was happening and speaking to the President beforehand, Miller had prepared the groundwork for what, in essence, would be his appeal: the academic cheating by Sanderson was not Miller's fault nor did he attempt to cover it up. What he could not predict was the mood of the campus nor the sentiment of the people appointed to the panel. If they and the campus viewed him in any way as a bigot, his appeal would be short-lived. If, on the other hand, he came across as a reasonable person who was being unfairly maligned, he had a chance. That was his game plan.

The President appointed a five-person panel, with Bergman as a non-voting observer as Miller had requested. The chairperson was the Provost, Anna Stoyer, a German scholar of wide renown. Joining her was Associate Dean John Hemple, Professor of Physiology Max Robbins, and Ted Brown, a graduate of the law school, who was also Chairman of the Board of Trustees for the University. The fifth member was the Deputy State Health Commissioner, Irving Stone. He would represent the Governor, since part of the financing for the University Medical Center came from the state. The first meeting of the panel was scheduled in one week's time in the Administration Building on the Main campus. The date was September 10th, one month before Jennifer was due.

Jennifer's belly had become a perfect sphere. When Bergman returned home from the hospital, she was invariably propped up in bed reading, with the windows open and delightfully cool breezes whipping the curtains to and fro. She enjoyed the change in weather immensely. Her metabolism was in super drive, and her body was generating a considerable amount of heat; the breezes of early autumn were a perfect antidote. He stretched out on the bed, went to her, gave her a quick kiss on the forehead, and unbuttoned the front of her dress. She hardly looked up from her book. She knew it wasn't sex he was interested in. It was the globe containing his unborn child, pressing out beneath the flesh of her abdomen, causing purplish streaks to appear on either side of the umbilicus. His hand rested on her skin as he slowly massaged her swollen belly; he brought his hand to a stop at the height of the protuberance.

He waited.

"Be patient," Jennifer said. "It knows you're there. Be patient."

He nodded. What was the rush? Suddenly, it came. The quick little kick from somewhere deep in the swollen womb, under layers of amniotic fluid and uterine muscle and abdominal fat and skin. Quick little kicks. Small thumps against his hand. Signals from his child.

Jennifer reached down with her hand and patted the back of his head. "I told you to be patient."

"Does it bother you much, all that kicking?"

"Nope, not any more. I'm used to it now." "What do you think, boy or girl?"

She smoothed his hair. "Whatever. Doesn't matter anymore. I'm ready for it to come out. As long as it's healthy."

"Please God," he said softly.

They lay like that for a while before getting up and helping each other prepare dinner. The air was now almost chilly, and he closed the window in the bedroom. The curtains stopped flapping and hung prim and proper, as good New England curtains should.

When the phone rang at eleven that night, Bergman answered it expecting it to be the hospital, but at first there didn't appear to be anyone on the line. "Hello. Who is it?"

"One if by land, two if by sea ... and baby makes three," a voice whispered, then hung up.

"Is that the hospital?" Jennifer asked. "No wrong number," he told her. He didn't know what else to say; he didn't know what else to do.

CHAPTER

35

The President's Panel, as it was quickly dubbed by the university community, met in the board room of the administration building, on the main campus. To reach the building Bergman had a five-minute walk from the hospital, including a brief passage in an echo-filled tunnel under the service road separating the medical area from the main campus.

Once on the main campus, he cut diagonally across the area to the administration building and entered through a side entrance. The busiest entrance was on Main Street, which, as its name implied, was the primary road in the small university town. The road itself ended at the administration building, and there was a rotary for vehicular traffic. Main Street—at this part of town—was a collection of small shops that catered to students' needs: bookstores, delicatessens, pizza parlors, etc.; all in all, a very pleasant merge of town and gown. Once inside the administration building, he would take an elevator to the fifth-floor board room. There, leather chairs were grouped around a solid oak table, and large picture windows faced Main Street with the gentle hills of Western Massachusetts clearly visible over the low-lying shops.

The first meeting was scheduled for six p.m., so as not to interfere with the members' other duties, and he hoped this would become the pattern for all of the subsequent meetings. Six o'clock was fine for him, but it did mean Jennifer would be eating alone, and he was beginning to get uneasy about leaving her alone at night. What if there were more phone calls?

Provost Stoyer greeted the panel members as they entered the board room. As the second-highest officer of the University, she wielded enormous power but was regarded by both students and faculty alike as an eminently fair person. Bergman guessed her age to be at about 55.

She was tall and carried herself with an impressive bearing. She had short dark hair and plain, but not unpleasant features. By contrast, Professor Robbins was friendly; his nose was broad and, like the rest of his face, the skin was discolored by the lumpy residual of teen-age acne. Associate Dean Hemple and Deputy Commissioner Brown were both bespectacled, nearly bald men in their early 60s. Ted Brown, the alumni representative, gave the harried impression of an overworked tort lawyer, which he was.

What surprised Bergman most about that first meeting was how clearly the battle lines were already drawn. He had expected a certain amount of objectivity to be the overriding theme, at least in the initial sessions, but it was clear that both Associate Dean Hemple and Alumni Trustee Brown had already made up their minds as to the proper course of events. After Provost Stoyer's opening remarks explaining his presence as a non-voting observer, and after she discussed the need for a careful review of the facts as they pertained to the actual Sanderson cheating issue, Hemple said his piece. It could have been written verbatim by his boss, the dean, and for all Bergman knew, it was.

"Dr. Miller has done a great disservice to the medical center. He has given the appearance of foot dragging in his investigation of this disgraceful business and that is intolerable. With the Winchell Committee breathing hot and heavy on our necks, we'd be foolish to do anything but discipline him strongly."

"I agree," Brown said. "In addition to the medical center, we also have to consider the University as a whole. There are a lot of sensitive political issues on campus involving ethnic groups and minorities. Whether we agree with their points of view or not is beside the point. They are legitimate players, and they are crying foul over some of Miller's statements and actions. The Board of Trustees wants peace on campus. We don't want disruptions of any kind that mar the University's reputation and its image."

Provost Stoyer seemed non-pulsed by these seemingly rigid opening statements. "I thank both of you gentlemen for your candor, but I hope you will remain open-minded as the evidence is presented. Whether we should be considering the other issues that Mr. Brown has brought up is something with which the rest of us will have to grapple. Professor Robbins, what's your opinion about that?"

Robbins didn't mince words. "They have nothing to do with the issue under discussion—cheating on campus, fraud—so why discuss them?"

"I tend to agree," Stone added, "but can we really divorce this case from the other issues that were raised? They should be considered."

"Amen," Brown said vehemently.

"We'll see," Stoyer continued, "but first let's consider the facts about Sanderson. Whether—or how much—we branch off after that is for later consideration."

So there it was: Two members of the panel were ready to hang Miller even before the first item of "evidence" was introduced. That left a formidable problem to overcome. All three undecided members of the panel would have to be convinced that Miller was being unfairly railroaded. Miller had told Bergman that he expected the panel to call a succession of character witnesses to bolster his contention that his intellectual integrity was second-to-none. To assist the panel, Miller had provided Stoyer with a list of chiefs of cardiology from the most prestigious institutions in the country. But when she outlined a schedule for the subsequent meetings, there was unanimous rejection of the need to introduce such testimony, whether it be in the form of letters, videotapes, or audio recordings.

"We know Miller is well regarded by his peers," Stone said. "That's not in dispute. He could still be a cheater."

"Academicians just close ranks around one another, anyway," Brown added, a remark which evoked raised eyebrows from both Robbins and Stoyer, but no comments.

"Let's stick to the facts," Stone continued, "or we'll be here until Christmas."

"Alright," Stoyer decided, "no character witnesses."

Bergman swallowed hard. Miller was counting on just that sort of testimony to show the panel that he had nothing to gain from backing Sanderson's cheating, that he was above such actions, perched at the very peak of academic success and acclaim. Why did he need ten—or 20—more papers in the medical literature? He had nearly 300 in print!

"Let's begin with Dr. O'Brien," Hemple said. "He's really the key person in all of this, now that Sanderson himself can't or won't testify."

"I agree," Brown chimed in. "Let's have O'Brien come to our next session."

"Remember," Stoyer reminded them, "my intention is to keep this panel's deliberations confined to the issues at hand. That does not include a discussion of what is or isn't politically correct in Dr. Miller's behavior."

Nobody dissented, at least audibly, and after reviewing other procedures the panel was to follow, Provost Stoyer adjourned the first session. Only an hour had passed. It would turn out to be their shortest meeting.

CHAPTER

36

That evening's meeting was fully reported in the next morning's edition of the daily tabloid. It was never clear who leaked the pertinent information. Bergman suspected Associate Dean Hemple for several reasons. For one thing, it was in no one's interest but that of the medical school administration to publicize the fact that the recommendations of the Dean's Committee were now being acted on in the form of the University President's Panel. For another, the fact that the Provost had ruled that none of the "politically correct" matters would be pertinent was clearly something that the dean would prefer changed. What better way to mobilize public opinion than to publicize such news? And indeed, the desired effect was achieved. The Third World Student Association (TWSA) picketed Provost Stoyer's office demanding that these issues be addressed. How could she allow Dr. Miller's antipathy toward Asian- and African-Americans to be overlooked in any review of the Sanderson affair? For some reasons, the feminist groups never joined the protest—one bit of luck for Miller.

The relevancy or irrelevancy of such charges, true or false, did not seem to bother the TWSA. Its leader, a Pakistani graduate student named Mohammed Khan, was vociferous in his protests. His deputies, a Filipino law student and a Jamaican medical student, were less outspoken but equally adept at mobilizing student opinion. A sizable crowd of students had assembled at the provost's office by the time she arrived for work. She was not amused, to put it mildly. Although the statement she gave to the press was a gem of diplomatic evasion ("The students' concerns are, of course, important to us and will be considered in scheduling our activities. You can be assured that whatever is pertinent will be discussed, time permitting."), the withering look she gave Khan and his supporters left no doubt that she wanted as little to do with the TWSA as possible.

Someone else who was not happy about the turn of events was Miller. Bergman spoke with him briefly after a noon house-staff teaching conference in which they both participated. The house staff enjoyed these informal sessions probably as much for the free pizza and soft drinks as the didactic parts, and so did the faculty. Sitting around a food-laden table was definitely more comfortable than stand-up ward rounds, and the give-and-take somehow more rewarding.

What Miller had read in the papers was not the complete story, of course. The main item of interest to him, the absence of testimony from his colleagues, was omitted. When Bergman told him of that development, his face fell.

"I was counting on that," he said unhappily. When Bergman told him that there were already two votes against him, his frown deepened.

"Those bastards might nail me yet," he said, and Bergman could only shrug his shoulders.

The next meeting of the Panel was called for the following week. Several days before, Arlene Miller left a message for Bergman to please call her at home that afternoon.

"I'm very worried about Leo," she said, when Bergman finally found time to return the call. "He's really down in the dumps now. The spark he had seems to have gone out of him. And he needs that spark desperately. It's what keeps him going. It's what first attracted me to him. Do you have a minute to talk?"

"Sure, Mrs. Miller."

"Call me Arlene, please, I insist."

"If you wish, of course."

"Thank you," she said softly, then continued in a stronger voice.

"When I first met Leo he was doing his cardiology training in Boston, and I was there as a graduate student in Fine Arts. God, was that a long time ago! Believe it or not, I was dating Harrison Wentworth, who was finishing up a pulmonary fellowship. We went to a party in Cambridge and Leo was there pontificating as only he can on solutions to the world's problems—this was in the 60s so the world had plenty of problems. I listened, fascinated, and wound up spending most of the evening with him and lots of other evenings as well."

"Are the rumors true that his poor relationship with Wentworth is due to Leo's breaking up your romance with Wentworth?"

Arlene laughed dismissively. "Ridiculous. First of all, I never had a romance with Harrison—just dated him, and a lot of other young doctors as well. No, I'm afraid their problems had little to do with me. Whoever told you that story has a good imagination."

"So how did the feud begin, if you don't mind my asking? I know it was fueled by Charlie O'Brien's antics, but I don't know how it started,"

"Feud is the wrong word. It was all on Harrison's side with Smiley joining in later. Leo couldn't have cared less. I think it was jealousy, pure and simple. Harrison finished his fellowship, became a faculty hot-shot in Boston, and caught the eye of Jack Smiley, who had just been named the dean of the medical school and who already knew Harrison from their undergraduate days at Princeton—same eating club and all that. Smiley picked Wentworth to be his Chief of Medicine and after awhile he, in turn, picked Leo to be the Chief of Cardiology. Not only did he know Leo from their training days in Boston, but he also knew he was already establishing himself as a star. He thought Leo could help him make the department a big success. We moved to College Station in the 1970s, and we've been here since then.

"Much to Harrison's chagrin, Leo quickly eclipsed him in fame, which is the coin of the realm in academia, and it really, really annoyed Harrison. Especially since Leo never fit in with Smiley and Wentworth, plus being a war hero who was always defending free speech, a real gadfly. Harrison was a conscientious objector in World War II, a stark contrast to Leo's experience. The jealousy just got worse and worse, and Jack Smiley jumped right in as well." She paused. "Isn't it amazing that despite doing all the right things, your entire career can be ruined by an overly ambitious underling and colleagues who are such petty people that they're always looking for an excuse to put you down."

"No good deed goes unpunished."

"Exactly," she nodded. "But you know that Leo thinks of you like a son, Paul, and I think he needs your help again."

Bergman told her he was flattered at the compliment but what could he do? He was a non-voting member of the Panel and his comments could only be elicited by the other members, not offered spontaneously.

"I don't mean about the Panel. I've been reading about the TWSA protests. They've got to have an effect on the Panel. Leo's supporters have to do something to counteract them."

"Leo's supporters?"

"That's the point—who are Leo's supporters? I know who Leo's friends are, but his supporters? Who are the people willing to put themselves on the line for him? People who could counteract the image of the TWSA?"

One name came to his mind immediately. "Bill Douglas," he said.

"Exactly. But we need more than him."

"Arlene, you have something in mind, don't you?" She laughed. "There are a few people I'd like you to contact. They may be helpful. Hector Garcia, for example."

Yes, Bergman thought, he might be helpful by telling the story of how Miller had saved his life. But could that really do that much ...?

"Then there are two other people who were really close to Leo years ago who I'm sure would do anything for him. Jack Thomas, his war-time buddy, who lives in northern Connecticut not too far from here. And Lou Werner, his old football-playing buddy from Columbia. Lou's now President of the National Broadcasting System. The president of NBS can always be helpful. I'll give you their phone numbers. Please see if they have any ideas." Her surprising entreaty had come to an end.

Bergman realized the next day that it was fortunate that she had called him when she did, because the Provost forwarded a memo to all members of the Panel: Whatever transpired during the Panel deliberations was confidential. No one ("no" was underlined) was to discuss the contents of subsequent meetings with anybody ("anybody" also was underlined).

CHAPTER

37

The next meeting of the Panel had a different beginning. The campus entrance to the administration building was closed for repairs, and the panel members had to enter through Main Street and a gauntlet of pickets from the TWSA. The picketers said little, but rather let their placards carry the message: Fire Miller. None of the members were pleased by this reception. The fact that the meeting time and place were common knowledge was bad enough, but the realization that they were being pressured was not a comforting one. As they filed into the Board Room, Provost Stoyer stared angrily at Associate Dean Hemple. "I suppose we're going to have to face this crowd every time we meet."

"Don't look at me," Hemple said. "I had nothing to do with it."

The Provost's eyebrows shot up in disbelief, but she said nothing.

Hemple wasn't through. "The sooner we end this business, the sooner we avoid scenes like that." Robbins agreed. "I don't see any point in dragging this thing out. Let's stick to our agenda and take our vote and that will be the end of it, at least as far as we're concerned." The others nodded their heads in agreement. No one seemed to have much stomach for walking that gauntlet again, and Bergman had the feeling that the next meeting would be the last.

The session was initially devoted to reviewing what the dean's committee had already determined in their own investigation. They then went over summaries of the NIH and Congressional sub-committee reports that they had provided for the Panel after the University President had requested them. For Bergman, this was boring because there was absolutely nothing in the reports he didn't already know. The highlight of the meeting was the appearance of Charlie O'Brien. He had been asked to meet with the Panel, and he accepted the invitation, rather graciously Bergman thought, since he didn't have to be there.

O'Brien had become a pathetic figure by this time. No other lab would hire him and his contract with the University would not be renewed.

Provost Stoyer began the questioning. "We've gone over reams of documents, Dr. O'Brien, so we feel we have a good background for the events relating to the Sanderson affair, but we would also like to hear about it in your own words. We hope to establish guidelines to prevent this in the future. To begin with, wasn't there anything about Sanderson's action that troubled you at the time? And even in retrospect, could you perhaps remember something that could have forewarned you?"

A thin wisp of a smile played over O'Brien's wan features. "Dr. Stoyer, I wish I could say there was, but there wasn't. I was completely fooled by Sanderson, and I'm paying the price for it."

"Why do you think Sanderson was able to fool you so easily?" Robbins asked. O'Brien shrugged. "If you had ever met him, you wouldn't ask that question. He had a very forceful, engaging personality. He showed me his data sheets, his tracings, etc. Everything that he showed me was true and accurate. My mistake was assuming that the rest of what he told me was true also. But you have to trust the people you work with to some extent, and I guess I counted on his honesty when I shouldn't have." He looked down.

Hemple spoke up now. "Did you have weekly review sessions with Sanderson? Is that when he showed you the data?"

"Yes."

"According to the summaries we've looked at, after a while the raw data was omitted and you just went over summary sheets. Correct?"

"Yes. That turned out to be a mistake, a very big mistake."

"And when you went to see Dr. Miller, you showed him the data summaries, the tables, the figures, and so forth?"

"Yes."

"Did he ever ask to see the raw data?"

"No."

Hemple leaned forward. "Did he ever ask you if *you* had gone over the raw data?" O'Brien paused. "The answer is no," he said carefully, "but let me explain that there came a point in my relationship with

Leo, with Dr. Miller—about five years ago or so, I'd guess —where he no longer did that. He used to, but then he stopped."

"In other words," Brown asked, "he trusted you."

"Yes."

"What else did Dr. Miller do to merit joint authorship?"

"He helped us write the abstracts and the papers. Leo is excellent at that. Incidentally, I *asked* him to be a co-author. It's not automatically done, at least, not in our unit."

Stoyer broke in at this point. "Dr. O'Brien, we all recognize that Dr. Miller was far removed from the laboratory when all this happened, and I think we recognize that his responsibility in this matter is merely that of the division chief, but we are now concerned with his apparent unwillingness to pursue the cheating matter once charges were brought up. What is your opinion?"

O'Brien bristled. "That's not true! I was the one who refused to listen to Bill Douglas and Paul Bergman. It was my stupidity that delayed everything. Once Leo knew what was happening, he was on top of the thing like a clamp."

Hemple didn't seem convinced. "He delayed retracting the papers, didn't he?"

"Only to make sure the results could be verified. Otherwise, he would have retracted them immediately."

"Why are you so sure?"

"Because I know Leo."

"What will happen to you now?" Brown asked.

O'Brien shook his head. "I'm through, I can't get another job. No university will touch me with a ten-foot pole. I'll probably go to work for the pharmaceutical industry, which paradoxically will pay me a lot more than the university."

Bergman couldn't help smiling. It was ironic that the punishment for violating the rules of academia was to be paid better.

O'Brien was excused as the Panel discussed his testimony at length. Hemple and Brown were convinced Miller did not act properly; Stoyer disagreed. The other two weren't so sure.

Brown wanted to bring up the other aspects of this case, specifically the TWSA's accusations, but Stoyer refused, at least for now. Brown continued to harangue the Panel with the need for the University to act tough in this matter, and Bergman thought that except for Stoyer, the Panel tended to agree with him. "We should vote on this matter now," Brown insisted.

"Not in the heat of the moment," Stoyer cautioned. "We'll review the material again, and we'll vote at our next meeting."

"Which will be when? " Hemple asked.

Stoyer deliberated a moment before answering. She looked squarely at Hemple and said, "We'll probably meet again at the same time and place next week. I'll contact you to confirm." Her eyes darted around the group, finally coming to rest on Bergman. She said nothing, but her eyes seemed to be giving him some sort of message. It could have just been his imagination running wild, but he decided it was time to act. That afternoon, he made his plans.

CHAPTER

38

The next day, Bergman drove out past the confines of the medical center and its surrounding streets and was quickly caught up in the pleasant, easy flow of "country" traffic: people in no particular hurry to get where they were going and not caring who knew it. He settled back with the speedometer at a fairly constant 55 and let the highway flow carry him along. Music from the car radio played softly. After nearly two hours of this relaxing drive, he crossed the state line and entered western Connecticut. The town he was headed for was very close to the border, and in another 15 minutes he was pulling into the driveway of a small brick house on a street filled with very similar houses. Some builder 30 years ago had had a field day in this town, he decided, since the builder had left the stamp of his work on block after block of the town's northern environs.

Jack Thomas had said to be there at four sharp, and it was exactly that time when Bergman rang the bell at his front door. He answered it promptly, a tall, grey-haired man with the kind of weathered face one associates with years of outdoor work.

"Come in, young fellow," he said, and Bergman followed him into his parlor. The furniture was traditional New England, but the walls of the room were not covered with colorful seascapes and landscapes Bergman had come to associate with such surroundings, but rather black-and-white photographs of men in uniform.

"Sit over there," he said, pointing to a comfortable armchair, "and let's see what we can do to help you."

"It's not me you'll be helping," Bergman explained patiently—as he had done over the telephone the previous day—"it's Leo Miller, you'll be helping."

The wrinkled features smiled. "You know what I mean. Would you like to see what Leo looked like when he was a youngster? Here, take a look at this." Moving slowly, he peered over his wall of photographs until he found the one he wanted and gently lifted it off of its supporting hooks. With a soft sigh, he settled into the sofa opposite Bergman and stared at the picture for several minutes before handing it to Bergman. "December 3rd, 1941. By the time it was developed, we were at war, and I sent it back home to my wife. She kept all these pictures for me until I got back. Good woman, my wife. She never knew whether I was alive or dead after the islands fell, but she never gave up hope. Died about two years ago of cancer. We were married nearly 50 years. I miss her a lot, a whole lot." He thrust the picture at Bergman.

The picture was of the three buddies, the ones Bergman had heard so much about that night when Leo Miller rendered his soliloquy. Two were alive—Leo and Jack—but the one in the middle of the picture was not as fortunate. It was his neck that the Japanese bayonet had ripped to shreds. They were a good-looking trio, cocky in their battle-fatigues with their old-fashioned World-War-I-type helmets, the only helmet they would ever wear in combat. When the newer ones were issued, they were already in the POW camp.

"I got to know Leo real well back in those days," Thomas said. "He had a great mind, always talking, very idealistic. Leo was always sort of pinko, while I became more conservative over the years. I really got upset at him a couple of years ago when there were stories in the paper about him supporting the black agitator—was it Nakullah or something like that—trying to speak at his university. Where is that guy today, in jail?"

"No. He's in Africa on a commune."

"Humph. Good for all of us. Except the Africans." He laughed. "So what kind of trouble has Leo got himself into this time?"

Bergman employed the tactic he hoped would impress Thomas immediately. "It's a complicated story, but it really started when he refused to accept a medal from the Japanese government. He told me he had consulted with you and your American Legion Post about his decision beforehand."

The smile disappeared and a fierce, grim curtain descended on Thomas' features.

"The medal was for scientific excellence," Bergman continued. "Because it had the aura of a personal honor from the Emperor, Leo wouldn't touch it with a ten-foot pole. The administration of the university was furious. They were already angry at him for supporting the Nakullah lecture, but this cost them a million dollars that went with the prize and that was going to be the start of a new wing for the library. Leo didn't care. When it comes to anything connected to the Japanese military from World War II . . . ."

Jack Thomas nodded. As far as he was concerned, Bergman had said the magic words. "The Bataan Death March," he began softly. "The spring of '42. Those of us who surrendered were never the same again. It wasn't just that we were POWS, it was more like being concentration-camp inmates." He rose and walked to the wall over the fireplace. "Come here and take a look at these. They're from Japanese archives that were uncovered by our occupation forces in Tokyo in 1946. Official Japanese photos of the Death March, that sort of thing. There are movies, as well. My organization has copies of everything. Lest we forget. Lest we forget."

Bergman studied the photos closely. Thomas was right. It was like scenes out of a Nazi documentary. First the march, then the POW camps.

"So Leo needs my help. Sure, but how can I help him so it'll be of any good?"

Bergman had thought of what he would say on the ride over. He was ready.

"You're president of your American Legion Post. You're the National Commander of the Defenders of Bataan and Corregidor. Next week the committee that decides Leo's fate will be meeting for the final time. The people that want his scalp within the university are being helped by daily protests from a student third-world coalition group. We need a counterbalance."

Thomas scratched his head and looked at Bergman warily. "I'll be honest with you, doctor, I'm not exactly in favor of demonstrations, strikes, that sort of thing, but I suppose you're right. I'll be damned if anything less than that would make any impact on the kind of people you want to make an impression on. Well, I'm sort of reading your mind, I guess. I'm trying to figure out what you want me to do without just coming right out and asking you—which is sort of a silly thing to do, but then old age has it prerogatives." He thought for a moment, then fixed his gaze on Bergman once more. "Son, as long as I'm alive, I'll never forget what the Japanese army did to us on that death march and later in the camps. None of us who were part of it ever will. For me, part of that was Leo Miller. So I don't care what kind of liberal he is. If he told the Emperor of Japan to take his royal medal and stuff it up his royal ass, then I'm going to do whatever it takes to help Leo. And if that means bringing a bunch of old veterans to your campus to demonstrate, then that's what I'll do." He stared at Bergman with a crafty smile. "But it won't be easy, by God it won't. There aren't enough of us old codgers —the Defenders—around these parts to make much noise, so I'll have to get my American Legion post to help. Can't say they'll be too pleased. Most of em are Vietnam vets who are more concerned about Agent Orange than anything else; the rest are from Korea and always feel they never got the recognition the World War II vets got, and even now they feel they're getting second-classed again by the Vietnam vets who are suddenly everyone's darlings because of guilt feelings. That's one good thing that came out of the Korean War. So I've got my work cut out for me. But I'll do it. I'll find a way and I'll do it. I'm calling a special meeting for tomorrow night." Asking Thomas to call him with the results of his meeting, Bergman drove back home.

He started to tell Jennifer what he had accomplished, but she burst into tears when she saw him.

"I had a phone-call just now from the same crazy guy who's been sending me the postcards. I'm scared!"

"Why do you think it was the same guy?"

"He said the same thing the postcards did."

"I had a call like that too, a week or so ago."

"You did? Why didn't you tell me?"

"I didn't want to upset you."

"Well, what do we do now? Can't we go to the police? Somebody's threatening us, threatening me."

Bergman called the police and spoke to a detective for several minutes.

"He says it's probably a practical joker, but to keep records of when the calls were made, and to keep the postcards. Someone will come around to talk to you in the next several days."

"And what about you? Are you going to be around here more, just in case?"

"I'm going to Boston tomorrow to talk to Bill Douglas, then I'll come straight back. Please, Jen, don't panic but keep the door locked."

"You're a big help," she said sarcastically and retreated to the bathroom, slamming the door.

CHAPTER

39

Bergman met Douglas at a restaurant near his clinic, one of the largest in the city and affiliated with Harvard Medical School. Douglas was enjoying his work immensely. He felt he had been prepared well and his association with Leo Miller had given him an added edge when it came to cardiovascular physiology. He had been following the developments in Miller's case in the *Boston Globe*, but was surprised to learn that the TWSA's clout was as great as it appeared.

"They're too disparate," he said. "It's rare for them to act with one voice. I wouldn't be surprised if there isn't some Japan-bashing going on *within* the group. Mohammed Khan must be holding them together with threats or bribes."

"Well, what about the Black Students Alliance? It hasn't uttered a word yet. Any chance you can prevent it from joining the TWSA?"

Douglas shook his head. "Nope. If an opportunity comes along to line up with the other minorities against a white professor, they're going to take it. Period."

"But they respect you. And after all, don't they owe Leo one for the time he got Kwame Nakullah approved as an on-campus speaker?"

"Memories are short. Few of the leaders from those old days are still around. But say, I think the last president was Nick Johnson, or was he the one before that? Anyway, Nick's still on campus as a grad student. He may have some influence on the present officers."

Bergman leaned forward and in his most imploring manner said, "Bill, Leo needs help. He's going to get the ax the way things look now. If the BSA could come out for him, it would cut the rug out from under the TWSA—completely neutralize it. This whole "politically correct" stuff could be eliminated and the case considered on its merits. Leo would get a slap on the wrist at the most." What was left unsaid was that much of Bill Douglas' current and future success was due to the encouraging role Miller had played in his life and that it was not only the BSA that had an IOU outstanding, but so did Douglas. "Of course, I'll try and help Leo," Douglas said, as he scratched his head in contemplation. "I'll go see Nick Johnson, and I'll even talk to the BSA membership myself, if necessary. They aren't unreasonable if things are explained to them."

"Do it soon, Bill, things will come to a head next week."

He nodded. "I'll do my best."

The last person Bergman had to see was Lou Werner and that meant a trip to New York City. Jennifer reluctantly agreed that he had to go and promised to stay indoors while he was gone. After arranging an appointment through Werner's secretary, he drove to Manhattan early the next day, intending to return that evening.

The headquarters of the National Broadcasting System was in one of the awesome glass skyscrapers that line Park Avenue in the Fifties. Werner himself couldn't have been more hospitable. He saw Bergman on time and he listened attentively to what he had to say. His mostly bald head bobbed up and down in disgust.

"It seems like Leo's been railroaded," he said, after Bergman had finished.

"I'm trying to mobilize some support for him outside the administration building, as a counteraction to the demonstrations of the Third World Student Association. It would be great if I could reach an even larger audience throughout the state. I believe that the more people that know about his situation, the more support I can muster."

Werner wheeled around in his chair and faced the wall behind him. Like Jack Thomas, it had its share of photographs, as well as plaques for this award or that. He pointed to a football-team photo in one of the middle panels. "Our famous coach, Lou Little, loved him when he went out for the team in '47. Always the scrapper. We were both subs, but I got to play more than he did. He never complained and we became fast friends. Haven't seen him since the 40th reunion in 1987, but I sure am an admirer of the guy. You know what? I just got a great idea." He picked up the telephone and spoke to his secretary. "Ann, find Watson McKay for me. He's probably still in his summer place in the Berkshires." Watson McKay. Bergman was impressed. The dean of TV anchormen now retired about ten years but still in the news, doing special programs now and then.

"Watson's always on the lookout for some human-interest story he can sink his teeth into. Usually once a year or so, he comes out of retirement to do a program. Keeps his juices flowing, he says. This might appeal to him. Especially if I tell him it would be a favor to me." Werner winked mischievously, and Bergman had the feeling Watson McKay would not turn down the offer.

It took Werner's secretary no more than a few minutes to track down McKay in his farmhouse in the hills of western Massachusetts. Werner appealed to McKay's well-known sense of fair play and added that since the university was less than an hour away from his vacation home, this could be a relatively painless assignment. When McKay showed interest, Werner told him the network would borrow a crew from either their Springfield or Boston stations and send it out to do a remote from the campus. Werner smiled and hung up. "Your job is to let McKay know where to go, etc."

Bergman shook Werner's hand and thanked him effusively.

"I hope it helps," Werner said, and patted Bergman on the back. "Leo's got a good friend in you."

"And in you," Bergman replied.

CHAPTER

40

As he drove home from Manhattan, Bergman thought about the bizarre series of events that had ensnared him in this strange odyssey to enlist support for Leo Miller. He thought about the people he had met during this odyssey, from Dr. Bennett in New Orleans, still inveighing against the system that had besmirched the memory of her beloved house officer, Eric Sanderson III, to the members of the President's Panel, each with their own approach to the issue of academic fraud and political correctness. He also reflected on the fellows he had trained with, but had already lost contact with during this hectic third year of fellowship. Gus Adopolous was back in Ohio, and the others were spread out from coast to coast. What their feelings were about Miller's trial and tribulations, he simply didn't know, since there were no letters or telephone calls from any of them. They had left the area just as the scandal was breaking, and he realized that the news of the Panel's deliberations had not yet reached the hospitals and doctor's offices outside the immediate locale except, of course, for Boston. That would all change if Lou Werner's arrangement with Watson McKay held up. Television coverage would bring the Sanderson affair out in the open, for better or for worse.

When he returned home Jennifer was awake, reading. There had been no further postcards or phone calls and she was much calmer, especially after a police officer had stopped by to check on her. Her due date was only ten days off, and she was counting the hours as well as the days. Bergman filled her in on the results of his foray to Gotham, and she was duly impressed.

"Watson McKay," she sighed. "They don't come much bigger than that. I've had a crush on him for years. But how are you going to orchestrate this whole thing?"

"I'm not. Not really, anyway. I have to leave it up to the different players. All I can do is to alert them to the time of the meeting. The rest is up to them."

"When will you know?"

"Well, so far the meetings have all been Tuesdays at six. From what the Provost intimated, this pattern will hold. She usually lets us know by Friday of the preceding week. Tomorrow's Friday, so we shall see."

"Have you spoken to Leo recently?"

"I'm not really sure I should. No contact with involved parties, that's what the Provost said she'd prefer."

Jennifer nodded and went back to her reading. He made a sandwich for himself, briefly looked at a newspaper (mercifully there was nothing more about the case), and headed for bed with Jennifer in tow. Sleep did not come easily. Jennifer's question about talking to Leo made him think back to their last conversation over a week ago in his office. It had been a long day and Miller had his feet up on his desk, his head against the top of his swivel chair. A small but expensive portable radio, one with excellent tone, was on his desk tuned to the local FM classical music station. Handel's *Water Music* was playing, and Miller tapped his fingers in accompaniment. He had taken to smoking his pipe in the office again, something he hadn't done for years. Bergman supposed he again needed the calming influence of his long-time "companion." Miller seemed at peace with himself, but perhaps Bergman was deluding himself; Miller knew meetings of the Panel had already been held, and he knew it wasn't going to be easy. Out of deference to Bergman's status on the Panel, Miller said nothing about the deliberations but rather spoke in general terms about the implication of the Panel's conclusions, whatever they would be.

"Do I want to stay on here if the dean has his way and I'm removed as chief? I don't know. But I don't think I'd like not being chief. Too much time and effort put into this job to want to give it up involuntarily."

"What would you do?"

He smiled enigmatically. "The prospect of starting a practice at my age is not a cheerful one. Going to another hospital as chief? Perhaps—maybe a small community hospital, out of the mainstream."

"It would be a waste of great talent," Bergman objected. "You're a national resource."

Miller laughed. "Thanks for the kind words, Paul, but I think you're gilding the lily a bit. No, I'm afraid I'm no natural resource. Besides angering a few of my colleagues and research buddies, my demise will hardly stir any ripples. I possess neither of the two features that define success in today's world: power and money. In fact, I'll have very little to show for all my years of work if I'm unceremoniously booted from this job."

His great hawk-like face quivered in anger and, for a few minutes, Bergman was afraid to move. After he had quieted down, Bergman got up and left. There wasn't much he could say to console his mentor. That was the last conversation Bergman would have with him until the Panel met for the last time. Their paths didn't cross in the hospital, and he didn't stop by Miller's office. A few days after their talk, towards dusk, when leaves were swirling around the medical-school quadrangle in great autumnal splashes of red and gold, Bergman did see him briefly. He was struck by how much Miller seemed to have aged in the last few months. The investigation (inquisition was more accurate, he thought) had taken its toll. Walking slowly across the newly-cut grass of the quadrangle, his thick body stooped, hands stuffed uncharacteristically into his pants pockets, Miller had lost the proud, almost military gait of the past. The cool autumn day was the kind Miller loved so much, the kind that he said always typified New England to him, yet so deep in thought did he appear that Bergman wondered if he really noticed the brilliant array of foliage that leaped at him from all sides of the tree-lined quadrangle. Bergman stood at a distance and watched him meander along the gravel paths, past the ivy-covered walls of the physiology building and the library, moving slowly toward the iron bars of the West Gate. He watched as Miller ambled on through the gate, out of the quadrangle, and into the street traffic beyond.

For a few brief moments, Bergman was alone in the quadrangle. With the sun setting and the irregularly-shaped shadows of the four- and five-story buildings covering increasingly larger parts of the ground, Bergman suddenly felt very cold, much colder than several minutes earlier. Perhaps the temperature had dropped ten degrees he rationalized, all the time knowing that it had nothing to do with the thermometer. Seeing Miller so affected by what was transpiring had really saddened him, because he had imagined Miller was stronger than he really was. Bergman drew his long white coat closely around him and crossed his arms on his chest for warmth. He should have left the quadrangle but found himself unable to move. He was lost in a flood of memories of his innumerable meetings with Leo, mostly good times, occasional heated words, rarely anger. The last rays of the sun glinted off the tops of the buildings and flashed into his eyes, and finally he had to move.

Returning to his office in the adjoining hospital, he hung up the white coat and put on his brown tweed jacket. All the way to the car, he kept the picture of Leo fresh in his mind, for he wanted very much to talk to Jennifer about this non-meeting. The traffic on the highway was light and, as he sped along, he played with the dials of the car radio. Not until he flicked on the FM switch did he find what he subconsciously had been searching for: something baroque—Bach, or perhaps Vivaldi—he could not be sure. Miller's favorite music. Poor Leo. Were the newspapers right? Was disgrace inevitable? What he knew of the Panel offered little solace. It was definitely a "hanging jury." He drove rapidly through the twilight while the contrapuntal melodies of seventeenth-century music danced into the cracks and crevices of his worn Mustang.

When he parked on the street where he lived, an attractive six-story building in a modern development, he could see Jennifer waiting on the balcony of their third-floor apartment. She had seen him and was waving as he locked the car door, her face animated. Because of the chill now in the air, she wore one of his long cardigans, but still her swollen belly was obvious. She stayed in the chaise lounge while he ran up the back stairs of the building, let himself in the apartment, and greeted her on the balcony with a warm, wet kiss.

"My God, you're slobbering like a puppy," she said, pushing him away playfully, "but I sort of like it." Cuddling closer again, the pleasant smell of her freshly washed hair seemed to engulf her like a comfortable blanket. He ran the long, blond strands through his fingers while he kissed her again, this time with more control.

"I've decided you really do love me," she said, cocking her head to one side and looking up at him, very much the pixie. The end of the pregnancy was taking its toll on her pretty face, with its high cheekbones, soft but straight nose, radiant blue eyes, and pouting lower lip. All of her features now seemed weathered, tired.

He kissed her one more time and sighed contently. "I'm a very happy man."

"You'll be even happier when you can finally call yourself a father."

He grinned. "I don't know if happier is the right word to describe that feeling. Maybe fulfilled would be a better word."

They stood together on the balcony for several more minutes in silence, his hand resting on her abdomen where their offspring slept quietly for the moment, while Jennifer nestled her head on his shoulder. Across the street from the apartment complex was a park, and they watched the few remaining children at play, screaming, running, tumbling into leafy piles of multicolors, then being gathered up— protesting all the while—by parents insistent on finally sitting down to dinner. Like voyeurs at forbidden sexual rites, they watched the scene, almost afraid to be discovered lest they break the spell, yet too fascinated to avert their gaze. Soon, God willing, this too will be ours, he thought. Then the sun set, the sweet reveries passed, and with a jolt he remembered why he had rushed home.

"I saw Leo Miller today in the medical-school quadrangle, but I didn't speak to him."

"Did he say anything to you?" Jennifer asked, puzzled.

"No. I don't think he even saw me. He looked ... very distracted."

"That's understandable, but why didn't you say hello? Isn't that allowed?"

"Of course it is. That's the part that I can't really explain. Maybe you could help me with it. After all, you're the one with the training in psychology." His wife had more degrees than he did, for which he was justly proud.

She laughed. "You see, my education does come in handy. Okay. Let me think about it a minute." Shivering, she drew the cardigan closer. "But first, let's get out of this chill." They went inside to their one-bedroom apartment, rooms neat and tidy, furnishings, decidedly eclectic. While she prepared a salad of peppers, tomatoes, cucumbers, and assorted lettuces, she mused aloud. "You see someone you haven't seen for days, someone who means something very special to you, and yet you don't even greet him. That is a curious reaction."

"The way I rationalized it was that I simply did not relish antagonizing the dean any further, but at the same time I have to admit that I didn't have a great desire to rush up to Leo and say something cheerful. The bottom line is that there is nothing cheerful to say so I just stood there."

With the salad prepared, they sat down to dinner at the kitchen table, in reality a butcher-block fitted to a sewing-machine chassis. The salad quickly disappeared as they talked.

"You have such a unique relationship with Leo," Jennifer said, in between mouthfuls. "Of all his fellows, you're the one he thinks of as someone special, almost like the son he never had. That's what makes it strange for you to be on the Panel. It puts you in an awkward position. If you look at it in that light, it's not surprising that your feelings about him are still so ambivalent."

"Okay. Granted, but I'm still not satisfied with my reaction today. I should have gone up to him. At the very least I could have told him how well the pregnancy's progressing, because he's always taken a keen interest in you. No, there's something else that I'm missing, but I don't know what it is."

"Sometimes the reasons people do things appear obvious and aren't; other times things look muddled, but in reality are quite straightforward. Why are you sure that in this instance there's more to it?"

"A gut reaction, I suppose, nothing more."

She sighed heavily and shifted her weight. "I wish I could be more helpful, honey, but I'm just too close to the situation. I have my own opinions of Leo, and it wouldn't be fair to you to put my words in your mouth. So, my best advice is to ask yourself the question you have been asking me. Keep on probing until you're satisfied with the answer."

"Maybe you're right."

CHAPTER

41

That Saturday morning broke clear and dry, but the daily paper in the hallway left no doubt that beautiful weather or not, the storm had finally occurred. There, on page three, was a little box with a catchy title: Vote on Medical Center Prof to be taken Tuesday. The two-paragraph content had all the information one could want—time, place, players. Since the Provost had not yet called the Panel members with this news, it was not possible to accuse any of them of leaking it. Who did it was a mystery, but at the moment it didn't matter. Bergman spent an hour on the phone trying to find Bill Douglas, Jack Thomas, and Lou Werner to fill them in on the details. No luck. But since they all had promised to call back over the weekend with "progress reports," he knew he'd speak to them soon enough.

For Bergman, there were few more awe-inspiring events than the autumnal turning of the leaves in New England. For that reason, he and Jennifer decided to spend the weekend driving through the Berkshires, leaf-watching. They were not alone. Not only did the locals take advantage of the stupendous scenery, but so did carloads—and busloads—of tourists from all over the country. Hotel rooms were scarce, even in Boston! With Jennifer expecting in a few days and the Miller fiasco finally coming to an end as well, they knew this might be their last chance for relaxation in a while. Afterwards, at home that Sunday night, he aimlessly leafed through the Sunday paper while waiting for the "progress calls" to come in. The first one was from Bill Douglas. He did not sound too happy.

"The welfare of Leo Miller is of little concern to the Black Students Alliance," Douglas announced glumly. "No amount of reasoning on my part seemed to have any effect on the blockheads who now control the organization. And frankly, the membership in general isn't too keen on saving the career of a honky professor."

"Even one who spoke up for them when they needed it?"

"That's exactly the point I made, my friend. It didn't exactly fall on deaf ears, but the reception was not encouraging."

Silence greeted that comment. There was nothing Bergman could say that he hadn't already said.

"What will you do now, Bill?"

"I won't give up, I can tell you that much. I'm just going to have to call in every IOU I can and then do some creative juggling to come up with any kind of meaningful activity on Tuesday at six. That's when it is, right? I mean the time's been confirmed?"

"That's correct. The TWSA has been out every day in front of the administration building, and I'm sure they'll be out in force when the Panel convenes—the more counter-demonstration, the better."

"I'll try."

"I know you will. Thanks, Bill." Neither of them sounded too upbeat.

The report from Jack Thomas was equally disheartening.

"You know, Doc, I've got very few World War II vets left, and those that aren't in wheel chairs have no desire to do anything more than march on Memorial Day and Veterans Day."

"What about your Bataan buddies?"

"I've put out the word to all of those, east of the Mississippi. No responses yet. When is the meeting, by the way?"

"Tuesday, at six, as expected."

"I'll be there, Doc, even if I'm alone."

"Got any IOU's you can collect, Mr. Thomas?"

He laughed. "I got plenty, son, and that's my ace in the hole. Wish me luck."

Bergman wished him all the luck in the world.

The best news of the night came from Lou Werner after Bergman confirmed the Tuesday time. "Great. Watson McKay and a camera crew from Boston are ready to roll. In fact, he likes the idea so much he wants to do a few minutes on the network evening news on Monday, and then come back to cover the vote on Tuesday, and maybe even follow it up with a summary on Wednesday. Your university administration will get coverage it never dreamed about in its wildest nightmares. I just hope it helps."

"It couldn't hurt."

"Let's hope not. He'll be staying at the Manor House Hotel if you need to reach him." Later that night, when he told Jennifer about his plans for Tuesday, she laughed. "I think you've missed your calling. You're wasted in medicine. You're definitely an organization man. Wall Street could have used you."

They both laughed at that.

CHAPTER

42

Monday morning was another beautiful autumn day. Main Street seemed no different than it had on Friday, except for one crucial addition. A van with "Channel 10" written on its side and a satellite dish on its roof was parked near the entrance to the administration building. A television crew was checking out various locations in front of the building for good shot-angles. Four picketers from the TWSA looked at the crew with curiosity as they marched back and forth. Without guidance from their leaders, who were presumably in class, they looked bewildered. Were they supposed to preen for the camera, maybe shout a few slogans, or were they supposed to keep a more dignified "low profile?" Because the camera crew worked quickly and quietly, few pedestrians stopped to gawk and those that did soon moved on. After watching the crew for 15 minutes, Bergman too resumed his regular schedule. He was curious to see how Watson McKay would look in real life, but he didn't have the time to spare to wait for his arrival. He would have to wait to see him on the screen later that day.

Fortunately, Monday passed quickly. One thing Bergman did have the foresight to attend to was to call Bill Douglas and Jack Thomas to alert them to the expected footage on the evening news. He left messages on their answering machines; hopefully, they would receive them before six p.m. He also called Arlene Miller. She almost wept with joy at his news. "Arlene, it's premature," he cautioned her.

"That doesn't matter. At least he has a chance now. That's all I could hope for and you've given it to him."

He and Jennifer decided to put off dinner until the news was over. At seven, they turned on the set, tuned to Channel 10, and watched the pretty—but deadly serious—anchorwoman introduce the National

Broadcasting System's Evening News. The segment they were waiting for aired at 7:20, "Watson McKay's Journal."

The gravelly voice of the American heartland was known from coast to coast. He had been the NBS anchor for nearly 20 years before retiring four years earlier. Proposed for every elective office imaginable, including President of the United States, McKay had chosen not to venture into the political arena. He preferred to retire to his Manhattan apartment and farm in the Berkshires, his reputation for integrity intact. Periodically, his journal aired, and today was one such occasion.

White hair and mustache neatly trimmed, face tanned and wrinkled, he began his segment by saying, "I come to you tonight from the town of College Station, Massachusetts, home to the University of Western Massachusetts and its medical center." His backdrop was the administration building with the four TWSA pickets eyeing him warily. "What we have here, ladies and gentlemen, is a microcosm of the currents that are sweeping across college campuses and across our nation. I am talking about two issues that have come together in this pleasant university town during a gorgeous fall week. One involves responsibility for academic fraud, a not uncommon occurrence in any institution where research is undertaken. The other issue involves politically correct behavior, a subject not confined to research centers but to any institution of higher learning, including secondary schools, in the United States. The pickets behind me" (here he stopped and pointed toward the TWSA delegation) "represent minority students who feel one of the professors at the medical school has slighted them. The same professor is also charged with irresponsibility in not conducting a prompt investigation when cheating occurred in one of the research laboratories in his department. Congressman Winchell, the sharp-tongued and controversial congressional investigator with a large following, has jumped into the fray with enthusiasm. But can all of this be true? Can the professor in question, Dr. Leo Miller, an internationally known physician and chief of cardiology at the medical center, be such an ogre? Or is he the victim of a vendetta by students and administration, each with their own agenda of issues to be addressed?" McKay paused again. This time, the camera panned the entire circle in front of the administration building and then down Main Street.

"Tomorrow evening, when the special investigative panel appointed by the University President meets to vote on the dean's request for removal of Dr. Miller from his post, this quiet street will bustle with more people and more activity than probably has ever been in this space before. The Third World Student Association has planned a massive outpouring of their members to protest Dr. Miller's alleged anti-Asian and anti-black racist actions. These actions include turning down an award by the Japanese Government and downplaying the whistle-blowing complaints of a black cardiology fellow who witnessed the cheating episodes. Trying to counter the third-world students will take whatever friends and allies Dr. Miller, a respected World War II veteran, can muster. Each side will attempt to influence the vote to be taken by the Panel. That vote is scheduled for tomorrow evening, and I will be here then for another Journal report. Please join me again at that time."

We clicked off the set. "Wow," Jennifer said. Her face was animated. "So far, so good, Dr. Bergman."

CHAPTER 43

Tuesday afternoon, large-scale TWSA demonstrations were already underway. People entering the administration building had to elbow their way through throngs of chanting students. "Miller must go!" was their favorite refrain. The consensus among Bergman and the hospital staff was that the television cameras had brought them out. How could the TWSA pass up a chance for national exposure?

As the sun set behind the wooded hills, a slight chill was in the air on a beautiful autumn evening in the Berkshires, an evening that was dry and cool to the point of crispness. College Station would have been tranquil on most Tuesday nights like this one, with many of its older residents already getting ready for bed, but as Bergman turned onto Main Street he was dumbfounded by what he saw. There was no tranquility tonight. He stopped in his tracks and stared: this was no longer the quaint major thoroughfare of a rural college town with a university medical center in its midst. Main Street was now a hubbub of activity, but not the usual Friday or Saturday night frolic of inebriated college students behaving badly in bars, restaurants, or on crowded sidewalks. Yes, tonight the students were out in force, but they were nearly all sober and decidedly serious. The townies who had gathered to gawk at the developing carnival scene seemed awe-struck by what had happened to their town. The townies were a more varied lot than the college students: there were high-school athletes with close-cropped hair, spoiling for the chance to push someone (anyone) around, interspersed with farmers and shop owners and ubiquitous pitchmen out to make a buck. An ice-cream truck had parked midway down the block and was dong a thriving business.

"Hey buddy, you want ice cream?" the street-side vendor yelled. "I got chocolate, vanilla, and strawberry! Cups or cones, come and get 'em."

Another enterprising couple had packed a chest full of ice at one of the intersections. "Cold beer, get your cold beer here!"

Adding to the carnival atmosphere were the TWSA members—now 200 strong—marching in circles on the town green. The sense of spectacle was added to by the TV satellite track from Channel 10, the NBS affiliate. Bergman deftly pushed his way through the crowd and headed for the administration building.

If he needed any more evidence of Lou Werner's genius, he soon found it. One elderly woman almost pushed him aside as she shouted to her companion. "I seen him! I seen Watson McKay! He was doing his routine right in front of a TV crew not five feet from me!" She was thrilled. The most famous TV anchor man who ever lived had come out of retirement and was in her town now—tonight—in order to describe in living color the events unfolding at the red-brick building on Main Street.

Traffic was at a standstill as Bergman maneuvered around the milling throngs of students and town residents and an impressive number of visitors from the surrounding villages, always keeping his eyes peeled for the familiar face of Watson McKay, America's "most respected person" in poll after poll and, like the excited older lady, a legend to many in tonight's crowd. Bergman looked in vain for McKay's familiar, handsome craggy face with its distinctive white mane and mustache. When the state police barriers came into view, he stopped scanning the crowd and groped for his university badge, the ID that would allow him to enter the red-brick building and participate in the hearing, on this, the last of the Presidential Panel's sessions and the one at which the decisive vote would be taken. Even with the attention focused on them by the television cameras, the few pro-Miller forces aroused little enthusiasm on the part of the spectators. There were a scattering of home-made signs protesting his firing; Bergman recognized the sign-bearers as relatives or friends of Hector Garcia, the heart-attack victim who Miller had help save, but even they were largely ignored by the townspeople.

As Bergman reached the door of the administration building at a few minutes to six, a more dramatic scene unfolded. Because of the gathering crowds, the police had decided to close that part of Main

Street to vehicular traffic. Along the route of the double yellow line that served to separate north and south traffic, a small procession pushed its way through the crowd. Continuing up the center of the thoroughfare, and through the milling spectators, a small band of determined students marched with heads high. They were led by Bill Douglas and carried a banner reading, "We Support Dr. Miller." Underneath, in smaller letters, they had written "Black Students Alliance" and in much smaller letters, "Alumni Section."

So that's how Bill had done it, Bergman thought admiringly—a few kindred spirits and a newly created alumni group. Douglas saw him and gave a thumbs-up sign. Bergman smiled back and watched in appreciative amazement as the dozen or so blacks with him tangled with the TWSA.

"African-American Students for Miller," they yelled. And again, "African-American Students for Dr. Miller!"

The crowd of TWSA pickets parted in shock as the black students elbowed their way to the entrance of the administration building. Their shouts could be heard clearly over those of the TWSA forces which is how they caught the attention of Watson McKay. McKay signaled for his camera crew to follow him as he approached Douglas. Before he could reach him, the TWSA President, Mohammed Khan, ran up to Douglas, grabbed him by the shoulder, and wheeled him around.

"What the hell are you doing?" Khan shouted. "The BSA is with us. What the hell is this Alumni Section? You've got no right to be here with that sign." Douglas seemed to relish the moment. He went eyeball to eyeball with Khan while a hush settled over the crowd. Bergman could see that Douglas was waiting for McKay and his cameraman to come closer before he answered. Bergman could have screamed with joy! What a job Douglas was doing.

Not waiting for an answer, Khan turned to his followers and yelled "Ignore these people! They're misguided. They don't understand that the Jew, Miller, has disgraced African-Americans by making a fool out of Bill Douglas, the black cardiology fellow that tried to stop Sanderson's cheating."

Now it was Douglas' turn. He pushed Khan aside and faced the TWSA pickets. "Mohammed Khan lies," he shouted, secure in the knowledge that he had the attention of the television crewmen. "I'm Bill Douglas and nobody made a fool out of me, least of all Leo Miller, one of the finest defenders of free speech on this campus. And by the way, Mr. Khan, your so-called Jew isn't Jewish, or doesn't it matter that you don't have your facts straight? Facts were never important to you." The crowd of townspeople roared in laughter. Douglas had humiliated Khan to the point that Khan's followers didn't know what to do or say next. And McKay had recorded the whole scene!

Bergman showed his university ID badge to the guard at the door just as he heard McKay saying into his microphone, "A dramatic moment, ladies and gentleman. With the arrival of Bill Douglas, this anti-Miller demonstration has seen the wind taken out of its sails. I'm sure the impact will not be lost on the Panel members now convening four stories above us in the administration building." The camera panned to the Board Room and, sure enough, at the open window, faces peered down intently. Time for me to join them, Bergman said to himself, and once inside the entranceway, quickly found an elevator for the trip to the fourth floor.

The Panel members were all in the Board Room by the time he arrived, talking in twos and threes by the window.

Brown, the alumni representative, was still arguing that the TWSA was too powerful a force to trifle with, but Robbins looked at him and said scornfully, "If a handful of black students could neutralize them in five minutes, why is the Administration so afraid to go against them?"

The Provost also joined in. "Don't you now see this whole issue is irrelevant?" she asked Brown, but he wouldn't budge. Neither would Dean Hemple.

"So one group of students is for him and one group is against him," Hemple said. "Big deal. Look at those people down there. They're laughing at both groups! I don't see any regular folks rallying for Miller." The Associate Dean looked each of his fellow Panel members in the eye. "Do you?"

"That's not important," said Robbins, but at least one person seemed to take the alumni president's words seriously. The deputy state health commissioner, Stone, went to the window and stared down at the crowded street. Streetlights were turned on, and in the glare of the lights, the scene had even more of a circus quality that before.

"The governor was not too pleased with the NBS news last night," Stone announced matter-of-factly. "We don't need any adverse publicity for the university or for the state. This whole investigation is being blown out of proportion. Let's not overlook the political consequences."

"What does that mean?" Hemple asked belligerently.

The deputy health commissioner remained unperturbed. "It means we have to weigh what we do very carefully."

"Miller should be punished," Hemple persisted, and the alumni president nodded his assent. Robbins and Stoyer shook their heads in disagreement.

"A bad precedent," Robbins said.

Hemple went to the window and put his arm around the deputy health commissioner. "Irving," he said softly, "you said yourself you've got two sets of students facing off against one another. Okay, maybe there's no consensus one way or the other in terms of student reaction, but what of the people in town, your typical voters? Look down there. For them, it's just a night's fun. They don't give a damn one way or another. Christ, it's not like the American Legion was marching up the street to praise Leo Miller." As if on cue, a new addition to the Main Street circus announced its arrival.

Where he had gotten the idea of the pipe and drum, Bergman didn't know, but Jack Thomas had not only gotten the idea, he got the instruments. A piper on one side of Thomas, and a drummer on the other, and all three of them with their blue American Legion caps, they marched up Main Street playing "Yankee Doodle Dandy." Behind them came a half-dozen of their colleagues, also with blue caps, carrying their own hand-made banner. The uneven letters said simply: "Defenders of Bataan and Corregidor." Behind them, a second group of six carried another banner: "Support Leo Miller." Bergman was astounded to see yet six more survivors of the Bataan Death March alive and well. With Miller and Thomas that made eight in all. Once again a vague memory stirred of a family dinner a long time ago (a Thanksgiving dinner) when his uncles had talked about their war experiences, and his father had said that someday he might well meet a survivor of the Death March. Not just one, Dad, he thought, I'm going to meet eight of them!

The crowd parted to let the veterans through. Watson McKay spun around so he could face Jack Thomas as he led his forces to the administration building. The TV cameras honed in on the group. As the veterans marched defiantly up the street, the onlookers suddenly became animated. These were war veterans, POWs. The townspeople voiced their approval of the marchers and their marching song, some even joining them as they swept pass.

From his perch at the window, Hemple gasped and turned white. The deputy health commissioner said nothing, watching impassively, knowing the governor would be watching the same scene on his television set.

Provost Stoyer broke the silence. "Time to vote, gentlemen. Dr. Bergman, I think it's best if you leave us alone at this point."

Too stunned—and delighted—to offer any protest, Bergman made his way down to the street. When Thomas saw him exit the building, he signaled Bergman to join him.

"It took quite a job to get these old codgers out here tonight, caps and all."

"You're fantastic," Bergman said, in genuine admiration.

An angry Mohammed Khan and his two vice-presidents pushed him aside. "Get your fascist racist groups out of here," he screamed at Thomas as loud as he could, so that McKay's crew could pick it up. "Don't you know that Miller is anti-Asian?"

Thomas wrinkled his brow, then stuck his finger right in Khan's face.

Watson McKay slid next to Bergman. "Move back a little, please," he whispered, "I want to get a good shot of this exchange." Bergman did as requested. Meanwhile, Thomas had started to speak, and the crowd grew quiet. "Leo Miller has nothing against anybody but the Japanese military," he said. "They tortured him and our buddies, and he would never accept a medal from a government led by Emperor Hirohito that has yet to apologize for its actions in World War II. Now,

I'll tell you something, fella. It's not just a bunch of American POWs that have long memories. There are Dutch and British and Australian POWs with similar stories. And you ask some of your Chinese friends about the rape of Nanking, you ask some of your Filipino and Korean friends about life under Japanese occupation. Seems to me, fella, you couldn't accuse them of being anti-Asian."

"That's just a cover-up for Miller," Khan sneered. His Jamaican vice-president agreed, but his Filipino vice-president said nothing.

Quick as a fox, Thomas caught the young man's hesitation and said softly, "Something you wanted to say, young man?"

The Filipino's head dropped. He seemed to be wrestling with himself. Finally, he told the crowd, "It's true, what he says. My uncle died on the Bataan Death March. So did a lot of Filipino POWs. My father told us the story every year on Independence Day. Life under the Japanese was a living hell for all Filipinos, civilians, too."

"And your Independence Day is the same as ours," Thomas said gently, "July 4th, but in 1946 instead of 1776."

Thomas turned to his group. "Did you hear that, boys? This fella's a nephew of one of the Filipino soldiers who fought with us. God bless you son. Please, march with us tonight, for your uncle and all his buddies!" He put his hand around the youth's neck and drew him close. Tears flowed down the old man's cheek. "All of you out there, listen to me. There was never a finer man than Leo Miller. Don't let them throw him out!" He signaled his piper and drummer to play again, and with his arm around the Filipino law student, he paraded his troops around the circle in front of the administration building. Everyone except the stupefied TWSA pickets cheered loudly. Within a few minutes, the TWSA group had splintered with many of the Asian students deserting the cause; Khan's followers were now reduced to 50 or so.

When Watson McKay went on the air some 15 minutes later, he stretched his segment to almost a full ten minutes to include taped highlights of Bill Douglas' arrival as well as that of Jack Thomas'. Before he signed off, a security guard from the administration building slipped a note in his hand. Hardly breaking stride, he read it as he talked. "This has been a remarkable evening, even for a veteran reporter like yours truly. I've seen a few things in my time, but nothing quite as moving as the fervent response that Leo Miller's supporters have brought forth tonight. I've just learned that the University President's Panel has voted *not* to take any disciplinary action against Dr. Miller. What's the moral to this story? I'll let you, the viewers, decide for yourselves. As for myself, I'm just glad I was here. My visit to College Station has reminded me again what a strange and wonderful breed we Americans are. God bless us all."

In the background, a huge roar went up as the news of the vote spread: exoneration. The actual tally was never announced, but Bergman had a feeling Deputy Commissioner Stone had cast the deciding vote.

CHAPTER

44

When Bergman arrived home, he was surprised to find the door to the apartment ajar. Hadn't he told Jennifer to keep the door locked? Hurrying inside, he stopped short at the scene that confronted him. His wife was bound and gagged on the sofa, her eyes bulging with fear. Opposite her sat a bearded, slovenly hulk with blond hair cascading down his neck and onto his shoulders, and an eight-inch knife in his right hand. Bergman stared at the man who looked vaguely familiar.

"Welcome home," the stranger rasped.

"Who the hell are you? What do you want?"

"Don't you recognize your old lab buddy?"

"Sanderson?"

"Who else, you idiot? You see it's just like my messages said. One by land—that's you—one by sea, that's me, though I really came by the river, and then there's baby over here that makes three." He pointed the knife at Jennifer's belly.

"You crazy fool, what do you want?" Bergman shouted.

"What do I want? I want my life back and if you don't give it to me, I'll kill your wife and your baby."

"But how..."

"You got Leo Miller cleared. We watched it on TV. I want you to do for me what you did for him—get me cleared. You call your friend Watson McKay. I know you have his number. Tell him how you and O'Brien and Eddy framed me. Tell him to get on the air and say that, and I'll get out of your life, forever. That's all I want."

"But that's not possible..."

"Oh no? You want this knife chopping up your wife's insides with your baby in it?"

The look in Sanderson's eyes frightened Bergman. This wild, disheveled remnant of a medical scientist was deranged, no longer the person he knew. Even if driven once by ambition, jealousy, and even malice, that other person was still sane. This one wasn't. How could he reason with him? He couldn't, he decided, and a cold, icy rage began to consume him.

Jennifer made a move to the side of the sofa away from Sanderson and when he tried to pull her upright, Bergman knew this was the time to end the nightmare. He took two leaping strides across the room and landed on top of Sanderson. Hitting his arm with all the force he could muster, he knocked the knife to the floor. Swinging wildly at Sanderson's head, he made contact over and over while Sanderson grunted in pain, his face contorted and drenched with sweat. Bergman fell back and Sanderson was on him now, flailing away until a quick knee to the groin doubled him over while Bergman grabbed desperately for the knife lying between them. With one fluid motion he thrust it into Sanderson's chest, angling the blade so as to pierce the space just beneath the breast bone, then turning it up, up into the heart. Bright red blood gurgled around the stab site, then shot toward him in a geyser, and he knew he had pierced that vital organ, the one he was dedicated to healing, not destroying. But not tonight. Tonight he knew that as long as Sanderson lived, he would haunt them for the rest of their lives. Ignoring the pleading look in Sanderson's eyes he twisted the blade deeper and deeper until all body movement stopped.

Ripping the tape off Jennifer's mouth, he sat her up and undid the ties on her hands and feet. "Forgive me," he pleaded, but she could only gasp in deep labored breaths. "Forgive me," he repeated, hugging her tightly. "I should never have left you alone." She nodded weakly, but said nothing. Quickly dialing 911, he sat by her side until the police cars and ambulance arrived. As soon as she was loaded into the ambulance, her labor began. He rode with her as the contractions became stronger and more frequent. He kept on kissing and caressing her, but she was too exhausted to do more than nod at him. "I love you so much, Jennifer. I'm so sorry I got you into this mess. Please forgive me." Then in a lower tone he whispered, "I had to kill him you know, I had to."

She stared back at him, grimacing with each contraction. "I know," she said.

While they were prepping her for the delivery, he kept on saying it over and over to himself. He went with her to the delivery room, trying to remain composed, but scared for her and the baby. Finally, Jennifer bore down with all her strength and the baby's head emerged from the birth canal. Thirty seconds later, Jennifer Steiner Bergman gave birth to an eight-pound five-ounce boy—a healthy baby, the obstetrician assured her.

CHAPTER

45

February 1992

The winter snows came to the Berkshires in wave after wave of ferocious squalls, starting in early December. By February, many of the back roads in the Bergman's neighborhood were narrowed by sizable snow banks that lined the shoulders of the roads. On the second Sunday of the month, a sunny but cold day, Jennifer and Bergman debated whether or not they should venture out into the frigid air.

"The roads are probably icy," he suggested. "I'm sure Leo and Arlene will understand if we don't come."

"For heaven's sake," Jennifer said in her most exasperated tone, "the sun is shining, we have brand new steel-belted tires on our four-wheel drive car, and we promised the Millers we'd come, so how can we back out now? Where's your sense of adventure?"

He shrugged. "Bundle up the baby and let's go."

While Jennifer prepared their son for his winter outing, Bergman stood and watched the two of them. Jennifer had never looked lovelier as she took to motherhood like the proverbial duck to water. Then again, having a baby like Peter, didn't hurt. Two weeks after his birth, he was already sleeping long hours through most of the night, to their relief. Now, at four months, he was as bright and perky as one would ever want a child to be. His features were a blend of his mother and father, but his smile was definitely inherited from his mother. He was one happy little baby and they, in turn, felt themselves to be very lucky parents. Both sets of grandparents were enthralled with him as well, and between their visits to College Station and trips to New York and Boston, there weren't too many weeks that he lacked for grey-haired admirers.

The Millers had invited the Bergmans for Sunday dinner, ostensibly for Leo to discuss future plans in cardiology for Bergman, but really to play with little Peter. Because they did not have children of their own and since Jennifer had given birth to Peter less than 24 hours after the panel had voted not to reprimand Leo, he took the baby's birth to be a good luck omen, a change of heart for someone who said he didn't believe in omens. He had even attended the ritual circumcision the following week.

The circumcision was the occasion for the first large-scale social gathering of the faculty since Sanderson's death a week earlier. After the religious ritual had been concluded, the conversation quickly turned to the previous week's events. Why had Sanderson been living as a squatter in a deserted summer cabin on a lake, as the State Police officials had reported? Why did unfinished letters in the cabin complain about a conspiracy, led by the Bergmans? What had happened to make him snap, when he always seemed so much in control? As Bergman had hoped, after the state police had interviewed the two Bergmans, they concluded that Sanderson's death was justifiable self-defense and closed the case.

In the weeks following the circumcision, the three Bergmans became regular Sunday dinner guests at the Miller home, at least on those Sundays when they weren't visiting Peter's grandparents or being visited by them. The meals were great fun, but they also gave Leo and Paul a chance to chat in a relaxed atmosphere. They had a lot to talk about—and not just Sanderson's descent into mental illness. Although Leo was obviously pleased at the results of the panel's deliberations, and amazed to learn of the role that Arlene and Bergman had played in helping to counteract the TWSA demonstrations, he had difficulty putting the whole affair behind him. He had been wounded, deeply wounded, by the accusations. The dean, for his part, avoided Miller as much as possible, showing no intention of resigning as he said he would. Leo was convinced he was still plotting some form of revenge. Likewise, although the influence of the department chairman was reduced after Miller's "acquittal," Leo also knew that Wentworth made no secret of his continuing grudge against the cardiology division chief. All in all, it was not a pleasant atmosphere in which to conduct one's research and clinical activities. Or so Miller concluded.

"It may be time for me to leave," he said on that wintry Sunday as he poked at the embers of a burning log in his fireplace. He spoke in a low voice and gestured back at Arlene, which Bergman took to indicate that he wanted their conversation to be private. Jennifer, Arlene, and a squealing Peter were playing on the living-room rug and couldn't hear them anyway, but by his tone of voice and mannerisms, Bergman knew that this was something Miller had not yet discussed with his wife.

"What would you do?" Bergman whispered.

"Don't know. I'm too old and set in my ways to go into practice or look for a new academic position. I may just retire."

"But you don't really want to."

"No, I don't. But the dean continues to make life unpleasant for me, and Wentworth just adds to it. Who wants to work with that kind of crap going on?"

"But retire? That's not you, Leo."

"You know that my goal has always been to help patients get better either by my laying on the hands, if you will, or by research, or hopefully by both. I've felt that to be the highest calling in the world. I really do. I still do. Now, I think I'm burned out." He paused for a few moments to light his pipe, then, restoked the fire. "One of the nice things that came out of this whole business has been the calls and letter I've gotten from some of the people I've trained over the years, and from my colleagues in the National Cardiac Society, even Ed Smith. I'll miss that camaraderie, but I just don't have any fight left in me. As long as Smiley and Wentworth are around, life at the medical center will be frustrating as hell."

Bergman put his hand on Leo's. The poker stopped moving for a moment. "Leo, if you quit now, it means they've won. Despite everything that happened in October, they'll feel vindicated."

"That's true. I can't deny it, but I've had a great run and I think I've accomplished some good. Look, I won't kid with you. I'd hate to give up everything and retire. But what are the other possibilities? The President of the University has asked if I'd be interested in the deanship when Smiley finally leaves. Great. How will the faculty accept me after what I've been through? I'm tainted goods. No, that won't work either. Maybe I should just take off awhile, tour the world, relax. Paul, I know there's one thing I've got to do before I die: I've got to go back to Bataan. Maybe this is the time to do it, to walk some of those miles again, listen to those far-away voices telling me not to forget, but not to keep hating either. That's what I remember most about Major Larsen, God rest his soul."

There was a gleam in his eye when he said "Bataan," and Bergman knew right then and there that Miller was going to go back to Bataan. "If you're not going to stay on as chief, then perhaps I should consider leaving as well."

Miller poked half-heartedly at the fire. "Once I step down, there will certainly be a transition period before the new division chief is named. It might not be the best time for a junior faculty member to join the staff. Would you like me to call some of my friends and see about a position for you beginning in July? Where would you like to go?"

Bergman thought for a moment. "If I can't stay with you, Leo, then I'd just as soon go to New York or Boston. That's where our families are."

"No sooner said than done. Now let's join the ladies and that little ball of fun you two brought along with you."

That March, Miller announced he was taking a leave of absence from the university. Despite the expectation of his staff that he'd return, Bergman wouldn't wager on his coming back. He saw less and less of Leo after that and aside from a wonderful going-away party at Frankie's pizza joint when the Bergmans left for New York in June—he had been offered a position at one of the city's leading medical centers, thanks to Leo — the social contacts with Leo and Arlene also came to an end.

When the academic year came to a close on June 30th, the Millers planned to start their trip around the world, as Leo had hinted they would. Before they left, Leo announced to his staff at a June 25th meeting that he was stepping down as division chief, effective July 1st.

Over the summer and into the fall, the Bergmans received postcards from all sorts of exotic places as the Millers traveled through

Europe, the Middle East, and finally the Far East. On Peter's first birthday, Leo called from Manila. "A special birthday call in honor of the boy. I'm going to walk Bataan all over again, 50 years later."

"Are you in shape for it, Leo?"

"As good as I'll ever be. Arlene's going to drive along behind me with food and water. And don't worry, I'll take it nice and slow. I'm not going to walk the whole way; I'll ride some of it. Should take me a couple of days."

"Anyone walking with you?"

"Yup. A couple of my comrades who can still walk on their own. Not too many of them left. Jack Thomas will be there, just like 50 years ago. We're going to start at Mariveles and wind up in San Fernando. Sixty or so miles of heat and dust, but no Japanese guards this time. Hey, where's that little fellow? Put him on the phone."

"His mother just brought him back from a walk and is trying to get him to nap."

"Well, give him a kiss from Uncle Leo. Arlene sends her best, too. So long, Paul."

There was something in Miller's tone that troubled him "You sure you're alright, Leo?"

There was a long pause before Miller responded, his mood suddenly changed. "I think so, just a bit anxious, maybe depressed too. I wake up in the middle of the night with my heart racing and my pajamas drenched in perspiration. I lie there wondering if it's all been for nothing, my years of work at the hospital. That's what this past year has done to me. Left me with three a.m. demons. When those demons are out, I sometimes wonder about myself. What kind of person would let a friend like Takashi Yamomoto be humiliated? Why didn't I signal him that I didn't want to be considered for the prize? I'm not the good person you think I am, Paul. I think I could have strangled Sanderson with my bare hands if you hadn't killed him. I'm not a good person."

"But that's silly . . . "

"Is it? Maybe I know deep down that it is, but it still wakes me up night after night." His voice lightened. "Don't worry Paul, I'll get over it. Take care." He hung up before Bergman could reply.

A part of Bergman wanted to tell his mentor that he wasn't the only one with demons. He wanted to explain to Miller all over again that he had to kill Sanderson, that he really had no choice. Even though he knew in his heart Miller would understand, Bergman was glad Miller had hung up before he had a chance to unburden himself. Leo had enough on his mind. He didn't need to add Bergman's demons to his. Not on Bataan. Not anywhere.

Epilogue

Bergman adjusted the volume of the TV set so that it wouldn't wake Peter sleeping in his room at the other end of the apartment. Outside, the muffled sounds of New York City traffic provided a barely perceptible background hum.

"Jen, come in and take a seat. Watson McKay's about to begin."

"Coming." Dishcloth still in her hand, Jennifer joined her husband in their den as the introductory music ended and McKay's characteristic tones filled the room.

"Good evening and welcome to this special NBS documentary on Leo Miller's return to Bataan." As he spoke, the cameras panned to the line of aged veterans walking slowly along the side of the highway that ran from Mariveles to Balanga, the dusty road it replaced long gone.

"This ritual of remembrance has been going as well as can be expected considering the age of the marchers," McKay continued. "They're hot and sweaty with aching knees and sore feet, but right on schedule. Before they left Mariveles, they ran into a group of tourists, among them British and Aussie war veterans who were used by the Japanese to build the railroad bridges in Burma when they were POWs. They told Miller and his crew what a wonderful thing they were doing by reminding the world about those days. Some of them were on the verge of tears as we'll show you a little later. But first let's have a word with Leo Miller and Jack Thomas, friends since 1942."

The camera focused on the two old comrades as they stopped for a moment on the outskirts of Balanga.

"You know, Jack, this is near where Dave Merrigan died," Miller said as Thomas nodded. "God, it seems like yesterday, doesn't it? I'm glad we're here to honor his life and the lives of all the American and Filipino POWs who died here so long ago, I really am."

"So am I, Leo," a tearful Thomas said, putting his arm around Miller. Their embrace dissolved into familiar black-and-white scenes of World War II, and the voice of Watson McKay narrated the story of how America entered the war over 50 years earlier.

"Leo seems happy," Jennifer said, leaning over Bergman's shoulder.

"Contented is probably a better description. I just hope he's made peace with his demons."

Jennifer sat down next to him, she put her arm through his and squeezed lightly. "Time for him to move on, Paul," she said softly. "Time for you too. All of us."

He wanted to say something about Sanderson, but thought better of it. He agreed with Jennifer. Time to move on.

Made in the USA
Lexington, KY
01 June 2013